CPACP

W9-CFY-062

It was rough and wild, hungry and desperate...

Flash loved it. She loved it as much as she loved Ian, and the only thing she hated was that she was too scared to tell him that. He made her feel too much.

They stood by the wall, their bodies still joined as Ian rested his forehead on her shoulder.

"I'm never like this with anyone but you," he said as he caught his breath. She loved hearing him out of breath. "You bring out the worst in me. Or the best. Can't tell sometimes."

"I bring out the you in you."

"You like me like this, don't you?"

She loved him like this. But she couldn't say that. It was on the tip of her tongue, but she couldn't quite get it out.

"More than you know, Ian."

Maybe more than he'd ever know.

1

Dear Reader,

If you're anything like me, you love the '80s movie *Flashdance* but always thought it was missing a little something—namely a holiday romance, right? As soon as I started writing *One Hot December* and I made my heroine a welder, I knew I had to name her Flash in honor of *Flashdance*. And, of course, I had to work in the word *maniac* in the story just once, because I am a child of the '80s and always will be.

The actual inspiration for *One Hot December* came from a writer friend of mine who is Jewish and married to a Christian. They celebrate both Hanukkah and Christmas, as many interfaith couples do. She said it's nearly impossible to find a romance novel that includes both holidays. So here ya go, Sara. This book's for you. And of course, it's for all my readers who celebrate Hanukkah and Christmas. I hope you enjoy the story of Flash and Ian and their romance that will last long after their hot December together.

Happy Hanukkah! Merry Christmas! All my best holiday wishes to one and all, no matter what you celebrate. Even if you celebrate neither holiday, we can certainly celebrate love and romance together, and we can do it all year long.

Tiffany Reisz

Tiffany Reisz

One Hot December

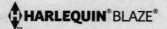

Recycling programs
for this product may
not exist in your area.

ISBN-13: 978-0-373-79924-4

One Hot December

Copyright © 2016 by Tiffany Reisz

Printed in U.S.A.

HARLEQUIN®
www.Harlequin.com

Tiffany Reisz is a multi-award-winning and bestselling author. She lives on Mount Hood in Oregon in her secret volcanic lair with her husband, author Andrew Shaffer, two cats and twenty sock monkeys named Gerald. Find her online at tiffanyreisz.com.

Books by Tiffany Reisz

Harlequin Blaze

Men at Work

Her Halloween Treat
Her Naughty Holiday

MIRA Books

The Original Sinners Series

The White Years

*

The Queen
The Virgin
The King
The Saint

The Red Years

*

The Mistress
The Prince
The Angel
The Siren

To get the inside scoop on Harlequin Blaze and its talented writers, visit Facebook.com/BlazeAuthors.

All backlist available in ebook format.

Visit the Author Profile page at Harlequin.com for more titles.

Dedicated to...

Sara and Sara and Flash

Acknowledgments

Writing the Men at Work holiday trilogy for Harlequin Blaze has been the writing highlight of my year. I've had so much fun writing these books. I can only hope my readers have half as much fun reading them as I've had writing them.

A huge thank you to my editor Kathleen Scheibling for her enthusiasm about the books. Working with you has been a true pleasure, Kathleen. I knew when I saw you collected sock monkeys, too, that we would get along just fine. Thank you to the entire Harlequin Blaze team for all their work on the edits and cover and marketing.

Thank you to my agent, Sara Megibow, for not only encouraging me to write the books, but for helping me get all the Hanukkah stuff right in *One Hot December*. I couldn't have done it without you.

Thank you to my beta readers, Jennifer Rosen and Robin Becht, for your great notes.

And thank you, of course, to my husband, author Andrew Shaffer, who makes it very easy for me to write happy-ever-afters.

1

VERONICA "FLASH" REDDING slammed her locker door shut for the last time. She pulled on her leather bomber jacket and popped her collar to hide the red welt on the side of her neck. Trading her steel-toed work boots for bright red Pumas, she put the boots in her backpack, slung her backpack over her shoulder and took a quick steadying breath. She could do this. More importantly, she had to do this. She would have told herself to "man up" but with the way the men in her life were behaving lately, manning up would be a step down. She'd have to woman up instead.

She found her boss, Ian Asher, standing behind his desk, poring over a set of blueprints for their next construction project—a small and desperately needed medical clinic in the rural Mount Hood area. A handsome thirtysomething black man stood next to him—had to be Drew, their recently hired project manager. She listened as he listed off changes they'd have to make to comply with new building regulations that might pass the Oregon legislature next year. Flash stood in the doorway while she waited for them to acknowledge her existence. Considering how good Ian had gotten at ignoring her, this might take a while.

"What if these regs don't pass?" Drew asked Ian. "You really want to redo the whole plan to comply with building codes that aren't even on the books yet?"

"They'll be on the books," Ian replied.

"You sure?"

"He's sure," Flash said from the doorway.

Ian glanced up from the blueprints and glared at her.

"Flash, how can we help you?" Ian asked. He did not look happy to see her.

"Our boss's dad is a state senator," Flash said, ignoring Ian to speak to Drew. "That's how he knows the codes will probably pass."

"If we don't build it to the new codes and they go through, then we'll have to retrofit it next year," Ian said. "We're going to do it right the first time. And my father has nothing to do with it."

"What's the deal with all the new regs, anyway?" Drew asked. "Four bolts per step? And that's a lot of steel reinforcements for a one-story medical clinic."

"You moved here from the East Coast, right?" Flash asked.

"DC," Drew said. "Why?"

"You know you're standing on a volcano, right?" Flash asked. "And not a dormant volcano, either."

"Stop trying to scare the new guy, Flash," Ian said, his strong jaw set so tight she almost heard his teeth grinding.

"Scare me?" Drew scoffed. "What's going on?"

"We're overdue for a massive earthquake in the Pacific Northwest," she continued. "And not your average massive earthquake. I'm talking the sort of earthquake that they make disaster movies about starring The Rock."

Drew's eyes widened hugely, and Flash grinned fiendishly in reply. She knew she was grinning fiendishly because she'd practiced that grin in the mirror.

"Is that true?" Drew asked Ian.

"We're in a safe zone here," Ian said. "*Safer.* It's the coast that'll get hit the hardest."

"Yeah, we'll be fine on the mountain," Flash said. "Unless the earthquake triggers the volcano to erupt."

"I…" Drew gathered up the blueprints. "I'll just go call the architect. Now. Right now."

"I can weld your desk to the floor if you want," she said as Drew pushed past her and walked down the hall at a brisk clip. "My treat!" she called after him.

"You're a horrible person," Ian said when they were alone in his office.

"Hazing the newbies is what we do. You want me to remind you how the guys hazed me when I started here?" she asked. "I mean, it was nice of the boys to build me that tampon caddy for my locker in the shape of a tampon, but did they really have to make it five feet tall and carve my name into it?"

"Yeah, they're lucky they have their jobs after that stunt." Ian sat down in his desk chair. "You got them back good enough, didn't you?"

"You mean when I welded their lockers shut with all their stuff inside?"

"Yes," he said, glaring at her again. Or still. Glaring had been his default expression around her for the past six months. "That's what I mean."

Ian was a gorgeous man and when she got on his bad side—which was often—she had to count to ten to keep herself from begging him to throw her down on the desk, rip his tie off, shove it in her mouth and do things to her body that it didn't know it wanted done to it yet.

"Safe to say we called it even after that," she said.

"They didn't do something else to you, did they?" Ian asked, running one hand through his sandy blond hair to pull it off his forehead. He needed a trim. She liked it longer, especially when it fell across his eyes while bending over to look at blueprints. But if Mr. Ian "Bossman" Asher wanted his hair to match the fancy suits he wore, he should probably tidy up. "I thought things—"

"The guys and I are good now," she said. "I haven't had to weld anyone's car door shut in months."

"Thank God. You are a lawsuit waiting to happen."

"Because I'm the only woman on your crew?"

"Because you're a maniac."

"Do you call all the women who don't like you 'maniacs?' Does it make you feel better about yourself?" She crossed her arms over her chest, leaned casually in the doorway. She felt anything but casual around Ian Asher, but he didn't need to know that.

He didn't say anything for a moment. Then he nodded. "You're right. That wasn't fair of me," he said, sitting forward at his desk and clasping his hands. His jaw was set tight like it usually was when she stepped into a room. "I'm sorry I said that."

She shrugged. "It's all right. After you fucked me and dumped me, I called you every name in the book and invented a few of my own. You can call me a 'maniac' if you want."

Ian stood up immediately, walked—almost ran— to his office door, pulled her inside and shut the door behind them.

"Can you keep your voice down?" he asked. "I'm trying to run a reputable company here."

"Then why did you hire me?" she asked.

"I didn't hire you. My father did."

"Oh, yeah. Then why haven't you fired me?"

"Because you're very good at what you do."

"You're not so bad yourself," she said with a wink. Since she had nothing to lose anymore, she turned and sat down on the top of his desk.

"I wasn't talking about that night."

She crossed her legs, which was hard to do in loose canvas pants but she made it work.

"Oh... 'That Night.' It has a name. I'm so good in bed our one night together has a name."

"That Stupid Night," he said. "That Drunk Night."

"We weren't drunk. You'd had two beers and I had two shots of whiskey and neither one of us is a lightweight. Don't blame booze for your own bad decisions," she said, raising her chin. "Or *was* it a bad decision? You tell me."

"Yes, it was. That I'm having this conversation with you is proof it was a bad decision. I don't want to be having this conversation with any of my employees. I'm trying to be a good boss here. You're not helping."

"How am I not helping?" she asked.

"Because you don't want me to be a good boss."

Flash almost felt bad for him. Almost. He was rich, he was handsome, he had been handed a high-paying job at a multimillion-dollar construction company with a bow tied around it, compliments of Daddy, so it was really hard for her to muster up any sympathy for the man. If he ever had a real problem in his life, it sure as hell wasn't her.

Then again he was also six-two, broad-shouldered, and annoyingly good in bed. She knew that for a fact thanks to "That Night" six months ago. And that meant she did feel for him a little bit. A little teeny tiny bit. Not that she would tell him that. He didn't need to know she liked him. In fact, the less he knew about that, the better.

"Poor Ian," she said, shaking her head. "A victim of desire. You're a Lifetime movie. Can we get Chris Hemsworth to play you? You two have the same hair. And the same shoulders. I remember because I've bitten them."

"You've bitten Chris Hemsworth's shoulders?"

"A lady never bites and tells. Too bad I'm not a lady."

"Flash." He started to cross his arms over his chest but then seemingly thought better of it. Instead he stuffed his hands into his pockets, as if they'd be safer there.

"Ian."

"You aren't supposed to call me Ian. When you call me Ian people start to think we are more to each other than boss and employee."

"Once upon a time I hopped into your shower to wash your semen off my back after you put it there after some very intense doggy-style fucking. Now...tell me again how we're just boss and employee."

"You," he said.

"Me."

"Why do I put up with this?" he asked. "Some kind of latent masochism, right?"

"It's the hair, isn't it?" She ran her fingers up her short scarlet red hair, spiking it even higher. It was a classic punk look according to Suzette, the multipierced stylist who had talked Flash into trading in her long traditional locks for a short, wild razor cut two years ago. Long hair and construction sites didn't go well together, anyway. Plus she liked scaring the old-timers at work, who still thought any woman with hair shorter than her shoulders was a lesbian or a communist. Not that she minded be mistaken for a lesbian. They were half-right, anyway. But a communist? Oh, please. Socialist, maybe, but a communist? Ridiculous.

"What do you want?" he asked. "Please tell me and leave my office so I can, you know, do what I do."

"Masturbate while thinking about me?"

"Flash, please." He looked so wildly uncomfortable right now she almost laughed out loud. Not often a man as strong and as handsome and as together as Ian Asher looked self-conscious. It was kind of adorable. Which made it so much fun to torture him like this.

"You know that's not my real name. My name is Veronica. You can say it. You called me Veronica that night. I mean, 'That Night,'" she said, putting the words into finger quotes.

"Everyone calls you Flash."

"You called me Veronica when you were inside me."

"Flash, dammit…"

"Dammit isn't my name, either. Say my name and I'll tell you why I'm here."

"Flash, I'm not—"

"Say my name and I'll tell you why I'm here. Then I will leave you in peace. Or in pieces depending on how much I'm annoying you today."

"Pieces is more accurate," he said. "I need to be steel-reinforced around you. You are an earthquake."

"That's the sexiest thing any man has ever said about me."

Ian removed his hands from his pockets, stood up to his full height and stepped forward, close enough to her that he could bend and kiss her if he wanted to. He must not have wanted to, unfortunately.

"Veronica…" he said softly, so softly it was almost a whisper, and almost a whisper was exactly how he'd said her name that one stupid night. Her plan to torture him was backfiring. Now she remembered it all…everything she wanted to pretend meant nothing to her. No pretending when he said her name, no pretending when he looked at her like that.

They'd gone out for drinks one night after work, about six of them, her and Ian and four other guys. The others were all family men, had to get home early. She and Ian had lingered at the bar, talking. But not about work, about art. His father had hired her, not him, and he hadn't known that she'd learned to weld because she was a metal sculptor in her free time, an artist. He'd assumed she'd picked up the trade from her father the same way he'd gotten into the construction business. She'd shown him a picture on her phone of the six-foot-high climbing rosebush she'd welded out of copper and aluminum, and he'd called it a masterpiece. And then he'd called her a masterpiece. And before either of them knew it, they were kissing. They'd kissed all the way back to his place and all night and here she was, six months later, still thinking about it.

"I quit," she said.

Ian's eyes went so wide she almost laughed.

"What?"

"I quit. This is my two weeks' notice."

Ian stepped back in obvious shock.

"You're quitting."

"I think that's just what I said. Let me rewind the tape." She feigned listening to a handheld tape recorder and nodded. "Yes, that's what I said. I quit."

"Why? Is it because—"

"Because you and I fucked? No. Don't flatter yourself."

"I didn't…" He sighed. "I'm not flattering myself. I know you weren't thrilled with how I handled the situation."

"You dumped me after one night and said you couldn't date an inferior."

"I didn't say that. I said I was your superior and therefore could not date you. You remember that part about me being your boss?"

"Only for two more weeks."

"What are you going to do?"

"I got a new job. A better job."

"Better? Better than here?"

She almost rolled her eyes.

"Yes, Ian, believe it or not, some people, like, oh… *women*, for example, might not consider working with nothing but men the ideal workplace scenario. I like the guys. We get along okay. But I like women. I would like to have some in my life. I would also like to have a job where I don't weld all day and then go home and weld some more for my other life. You can't blame me for that."

"I don't, no. You've stuck it out here longer than anyone thought you would."

"I had to fight tooth and nail to earn the respect of

the crew. I'm a little tired of fighting to be treated like a human being. You can't blame me for that, either."

"No." Ian nodded. "So…where are you going?"

"You know Clover Greene? Runs the nursery down the highway?"

"Yeah, Clover's great. I bought my Weedwhacker from her."

"I'm her new assistant manager. The pay is the same as what I make here but the hours will be better, the work not as backbreaking. I don't like going home too tired to sculpt. I've been putting my art career on the back burner too long. I don't want to do that anymore. Something had to give," she said.

"Your art's important to you," he said. "I appreciate that. I hate to lose you. We're not going to find another welder as good as you."

"You will. But you won't find one as fun as me."

"You put truck nuts on my bumper to punish me for telling you we couldn't keep sleeping together."

"So? It was just a prank."

"You didn't hang them on my bumper. You welded them on my bumper. Giant. Metal. Testicles."

"Your truck needed a new bumper, anyway, and you know it."

"Flash…" She could tell he wanted to say something but wouldn't let himself say it. Well, she knew how he felt. She'd wanted to say something for six months now. If only she could weld her mouth shut.

"You're welcome," she said.

"Wait, I didn't thank you for anything."

"I assumed you were going to thank me for leaving. I know I've been a…" She paused, searched for the right word. "A *complicated* employee. I know you'll be more comfortable at work with me gone."

"I'd rather be uncomfortable and have you here."

"I'd rather work for a woman I respect."

"Than work for a man you can't?" he asked, meeting her eyes. His jaw was clenched again, tight. She'd hurt him.

"I respect you," she said as softly as he'd said her real name. "I do. What I mean to say is…I'd rather work for a woman I don't have feelings for than a man I do. I shouldn't have made it about respect. I do respect you. I don't like you very much, but I respect you."

"I came on your back."

"I wanted you to come on my back. How would us having very good sex make me lose respect for you? I'm not a man. I don't lose respect for someone just because he has the bad taste to sleep with me. I consider it one of your finer moments actually. I respect you more for fucking me."

"I think about it sometimes. That night."

His eyes met hers for a tense moment before glancing away again.

Flash placed her hand on Ian's chest, over his heart.

"Welcome to the club," she said. She patted his chest and dropped her hand to her side. "I'm gonna go before I do or say something stupid. I've been known to do that. Examples include the truck nuts incident and that time I welded your desk drawers shut."

"Wait. You what?" He ran around to his desk. Every one of the desk drawers opened.

"Made you look," she said.

Ian hung his head, slammed the top drawer shut so that all his pens and pencils rattled.

"You're evil," he said.

"Just giving you a hard time," she said. "Gotta go, boss. I mean, ex-boss. Have a nice life."

She hopped off his desk and headed for his office door.

"What are your plans now?" he asked.

"Dinner at Skyway," she said. "Clover says they have truffle fries."

"No, I mean, you know we don't have any work scheduled until January fifth. Your two weeks' notice is kind of meaningless considering you didn't have to work this month, anyway. Are you starting with Clover next week?"

"Clover's is closed until March, and she doesn't need me to start until January. I'm going to enjoy the rest of the month off. It's December, remember? Baking Christmas cookies, decorating Christmas cookies, eating Christmas cookies, lather, rinse, repeat. Basically eat cookies all month is what I'm doing. And sculpting. You?"

"No cookies. Work," he said. "I bought a new house. A new old house."

"Cool. Where at?"

"Government Camp. An old ski chalet."

"Govy? You must like snow."

"Love snow. We have two feet up there already. Great view from my new kitchen."

"Sounds nice."

"It's a fixer-upper. I'm spending all month fixing and upping."

"A 'fixer-upper' ski chalet is still a chalet, Bossman. It's like saying you bought a 'low-end' Rolex or a 'used' private plane."

"Fine. You win. I'm a spoiled brat, and I always will be. I didn't earn what I have, but I'm trying to be worthy of it, okay? Which is why I didn't want to keep sleeping with you, because when someone gives you power over someone else, you don't abuse it. And whether you like it or not, I had power over you. More than you know."

"What's that supposed to mean?"

"Nothing," he said quickly. "I'm only saying I have the power to hire and fire. I shouldn't sleep with someone I can fire. I did it for you."

"Well, thank you very much for dumping me. It was very chivalrous. Good luck remodeling your chalet this December. You have to weld anything?"

"A couple things."

"Clean your metal. Acetone's good. If you don't have any in the house, you can borrow my fingernail polish remover."

She gave him one last little look, maybe the last one she'd ever give him, and left his office. She kept her head up and her shoulders straight as she marched down the generic beige hall on generic gray carpets to the parking lot. Everyone was gone. No surprise there. Last day of work before the holidays, and everybody had shipped out the second they could.

The only car left in the parking lot was Ian's new black Subaru, which she was pretty sure he bought because he couldn't look at his old car without picturing the truck nuts she'd welded to the bumper. She headed to her red '98 Ford Ranger, which had seen better days, trying to convince herself she was happy about leaving. And she was. She was excited about her new job. Clover Greene was about the kindest, friendliest woman she'd ever met, and she had a quirky green-haired teenage girl working for her as an office assistant—her kind of people. The nursery itself was like a well-manicured Garden of Eden. Everywhere she looked Flash saw inspiration for her metal foliage sculptures. Great people, safe place for women to work, nice location, good pay, good benefits and fuel for her art. So yeah, she was thrilled about the new job.

But.

But...Ian.

It wasn't just that he was good in bed. He was. She remembered all too well that he was—passionate, intense, sensual, powerful, dominating, everything she wanted in a man. The first kiss had been electric. The second intoxicating. By the third she would have sold her soul to have him inside her before morning, but he didn't ask for her soul, only every inch of her body, which she'd given him for hours. When she'd gone to bed with him that night she'd been half in love with him. By the time she left it the next morning she was all the way in.

Then he'd dumped her.

Six months ago. She ought to be over it by now. She wanted to be over it the day it happened but her heart wasn't nearly as tough as her reputation. The worst part of it all? Ian had been right to dump her. They'd both lost their heads after a couple drinks had loosened their tongues enough to admit they were attracted to each other. But Ian had a company to run and there were rules—good ones—that prohibited the man who signed the paychecks from sleeping with the woman who wielded the torch.

She pulled her keys from her jacket pocket and stuck them in the lock.

"Flash? Wait up."

She turned and saw Ian walking across the parking lot toward her. He wore his black overcoat, and combined with his black Tom Ford suit, he looked more like a Wall Street trader than the vice president and operations manager of Asher Construction. Ian told her once he'd started out doing cleanup at his dad's construction sites twenty years ago. Then he'd gone to college, come home, and clawed his way up the ranks the hard way: by working his fingers to the bone while learning every job. If only he was still just a guy on the crew, maybe it could have worked. Now when she looked at him, she saw a man with money, power, and prestige, a man completely out of her league.

"What?" she asked, leaning back against her truck door.

He stood in front of her, face-to-face, but didn't look her in the eyes. He stared off to the left where the peak of Mount Hood rose over the treetops.

"Ian?" she prompted when it seemed like he was going to keep her standing there in the cold all day.

"I need your help with something," he said.

"That must have been hard," she said. "Asking for my help."

"It wasn't easy."

"What do you need my help with?"

"A project at my new place. It's pretty delicate work. I don't trust myself to do it."

"What's the project?"

"The house has a stone-and-iron fireplace. It's what sold me on the place. But the fireplace screen is coming apart. It's nice, original to the house. Would you maybe be willing to come up and take a look at it tonight?"

"Has to be tonight?"

"You busy?"

"Would you be jealous if I was?" she asked.

"You have a hickey on the side of your neck that you're trying to hide under your collar. Not that I noticed."

"Except you noticed."

"Yeah," he said with a sigh. "I noticed. Who's the lucky guy? Or girl?"

"Nobody you know. Old friend from high school who moved back to town a month ago. We reconnected. And then disconnected."

"Didn't work out?"

"Do you care?"

"Yes," he said. He said it very simply. Just "yes" as if what he wanted to say was "obviously I care."

She shook her head, not at Ian but at her own stupidity for thinking she could have had something meaningful with this jerk she'd dated for a week.

"He was cute, he was smart, he was a good kisser, and he thought my art was awesome. But after a couple week he said he couldn't do it. He couldn't date a professional welder when he worked as a teller at a bank. His friends would never let him hear the end of it, he said. He just couldn't date a woman, no matter how hot—his words, not mine—who came off as more of a man than he did. I said that was fine. I didn't want to date a guy who was less of a man than I was, either. He called me a couple nice words after that and then he was gone. Good riddance to him and his poor little ego."

"You have to stop dating beneath you."

"I slept with you."

"Exactly my point."

She laughed. "You're cute," she said. "I wish you weren't."

"It's a curse." He grinned at her. "You know, you could have told that guy you weren't going to be a professional welder anymore."

"I could have, yeah. But it doesn't matter. I can't sleep with a guy I don't respect. A man who can't respect a woman doing a supposedly 'man's job' isn't going to respect a woman who does 'women's work,' either. I'm glad it ended before it got serious."

"You feel that way about us, too? Glad it ended before it got serious?"

"It was already serious before you kissed me, Ian."

"I didn't know. I had no idea you… It never occurred to me you had feelings for me," he said. "Except attraction. That I'd noticed."

"You look as good in your suits as out of them and that's saying something."

"Let me take you out tonight," he said. "Dinner. Then you can come back to the house and help me with the fireplace. We'll hang out. It'll be fun. It'll be normal. We can end things on a good note instead of feeling shitty about what happened."

"Or didn't happen."

"Or didn't happen, yeah."

"Do you even like me?" she asked. "As a person, I mean. I insult you, I welded truck nuts to your car, I scare the newbies and I make eighteen dollars an hour while you make eighteen dollars a minute."

"Dad makes eighteen dollars a minute. I make low six figures. I'm on salary, you know. I don't own the company. I just run it. If I screw up, I get in trouble or get fired just like anyone else who works for my father."

"Except the rest of us aren't senator's sons who are going to inherit the family business someday no matter how badly we screw up."

"Dad's only a state senator."

"And your ski chalet is *only* a fixer-upper."

They were silent a long moment. She knew he was waiting for her to bend a little, to say yes to dinner, to say yes to ending on a good note instead of on this... whatever this was...this awkward painful note.

"I'm going to miss you," he said. "You keep me honest."

"I insult you. Often."

"Somebody has to, right?" he asked. "Everybody else sucks up to me."

"That's the damn truth," she said.

"Please? Hang out with me tonight. Take a look at this thing in my house and see if you can fix it. Then we can go to the brewery. My treat. A thank-you for your help. We can pretend to be friends for one evening, right? Then maybe eventually we won't have to pretend?"

"Why do you want to be my friend?"

"You carry a blowtorch in your backpack and I had to pay five hundred bucks to get those fucking truck nuts off my bumper," he said, meeting her eyes finally. It was his eyes that had gotten to her first—a blue so bright you could see the color from the other side of the room, the other side of the world. "Of course I want to be your friend. It's safer than being your enemy."

She smiled, because she had to after an admission like that.

"Please, Flash. One apology dinner. I'm even buying."

Ian was strong and smart and it meant a lot to her that he wasn't ashamed to humble himself a little. A real man. He wasn't afraid of her even if he joked he was. Which is why she shouldn't be doing this, having this conversation with him, thinking these thoughts. She cared too much about him already. He'd crushed her before and he could crush her again. She absolutely should not spend any time alone with him ever again, not if she didn't want to get hurt like before, and God knows, she didn't want to get hurt like before. She was still hurt.

"I'll go get my torch," she said. "But you better make good on the brewery or your fireplace screen won't be the only thing I solder to the floor."

"You're sexy when you're threatening permanent damage to my genitals," he said.

She patted his shoulder.

"Tell me something I don't know."

2

IAN WATCHED FLASH walk back into the office to retrieve her equipment. Dammit, what the hell was he thinking? He was thinking he wasn't over Flash, that's what he was thinking. And he needed to be over her. He really needed to be over her.

And under her.

And all around her.

And inside her. He needed that more than anything else.

"Pathetic, Asher. Just pathetic," he muttered to himself as he fished around in his coat pocket to find his keys. Begging for crumbs from this woman when he wanted to feast on her. But he'd fucked it up with her so badly he knew she'd probably never lower her guard around him again. Not enough to give him anything but hope. Certainly not her love, which is what he wanted. Nothing else would do. And yet he knew it was over, all the way over. He'd had some hope when she welded metal testicles to his bumper. Only a woman with very strong feelings for him would pull a prank like that. But after that, nothing. Even the silent treatment would have been better than what he'd gotten from her. She'd treated him like she treated everyone else—with a mix of dark humor and utter disdain. He didn't want her to treat him like she treated everyone else. He wanted to be special. But this was Veronica "Flash" Redding, and if making men feel like they were nothing special was a game show, she'd go home with one million dollars and a brand-new car.

And today she'd quit her job. Which meant he'd likely never see her again unless he did something hasty, drastic and stupid like beg her to help him fix up his house in the hopes of buying a little more time with her. Maybe he could talk her into forgiving him. Maybe he could talk her into another night. Maybe he could talk her into welding metal wings and flying them to the sun. He was dreaming too big here. Unlike him, Flash was already out there dating other people. He hadn't gone on a second date since his one night with her. Why? Because he liked women and didn't want to be an asshole to them, and only an asshole would take one woman out on a date while thinking about a different woman the entire time. A woman with punk red hair, a perfect face and a body that fit his so well he could believe she'd been sculpted to fit him. She wore loose canvas pants every day to work and T-shirts with no sleeves that showed off both her strong shoulders and the tattoos on her biceps. She wore that distressed bomber jacket every day of her life, no matter the weather. Brown leather, not black leather because Flash wasn't trying to look cool—she just was cool. Too cool for him.

But still…he had to give it one more shot with this woman or he'd regret it the rest of his life.

Flash emerged from their office into the parking lot, a heavy-duty army-green duffel bag over her shoulder. With any other woman he would have taken the bag from her and carried it. But he'd learned the hard way not to try that with Flash. It wasn't the implication she couldn't carry a heavy load that pissed her off when he'd tried to be gentlemanly one day. She just didn't want anyone else touching her tools.

"You want to ride with me?" he asked. "Mine handles in snow better than yours."

"I have chains if I need them," she said. "This isn't my first winter on the mountain, remember?" She opened her truck door and put her bag on the passenger seat.

"My new place is a little hard to find so follow me close. If you get lost, call my cell."

"I won't get lost," she said as she slammed the passenger door and got in behind the wheel. "Lead on, Macduff."

"That's *Macbeth*, right?" he asked.

She looked at him, raised her eyebrow and then slammed her driver's door shut. Maybe now was not the best time to discuss the *Complete Works of William Shakespeare*.

"You're an idiot, Asher," he said to himself.

Ian got behind the wheel of his Outback and pulled out of the parking lot onto Highway 26. His construction company was located a few miles outside of Portland in Sandy, and Government Camp was a good thirty miles east, right up to the snow-covered top of the mountain. When they started their drive the temperature was about forty, brisk and cool, but not biting cold. As they climbed the mountain, the temperature started to drop.

In twenty miles it went from forty-one, according to the Outback's readings, to thirty-one and falling fast.

Signs of civilization disappeared as they drove. The little towns faded in the rearview mirror and soon there was nothing but massive moss-covered trees of Mount Hood National Forest looming on either side of the road. Then they really started to climb. The trees fell away to the right as the highway edged along a valley that seemed to drop endlessly. Nothing stood between him and that eternal drop but a low concrete wall. The trees in the valley were white with snow and the road's shoulder was piled high with the stuff tinged gray by highway soot. He glanced back and saw Flash right behind him in her little red pickup. As old as that thing was, he couldn't believe it still ran. But it did and it kept up with him.

Government Camp—a town that was neither a camp nor affiliated with the government—was on the left and he made sure Flash followed him into the turn lane behind him. It wasn't easy watching the road and watching her the entire time. He'd wished she'd ridden with him so he wouldn't worry so much. She was the most stubborn woman on the planet, easily. The next road had been scraped clean, but there were still four-foot walls of snow on either side of the street and a thin layer of ice underneath him. But he shouldn't have worried. Flash handled her truck as well as she handled her torch. No wonder she intimidated men. She was so skilled and self-sufficient a man couldn't help but feel a little useless around her.

But he'd spent one incredible night with her and knew a little something about Flash Redding—she did find men useful for at least one very specific purpose and he would be more than happy, ecstatic even, to make himself of use to her in that capacity again.

At the end of a long street, Ian slowed his car to a crawl, turned right into the driveway nearly hidden by snow. More trees—hundred-year-old evergreens fifty feet high—shadowed his house. He hoped Flash liked it. It wasn't bad to look at. A classic A-frame Swiss-chalet-style house with a green metal roof and cedar siding, it already felt like home to him even though he'd only been living there a month. It would feel much more like home once he had someone to share it with.

He waved her into his garage while he parked beside it. Before exiting his car he paused to take a few breaths. He could do this. He could have a nice evening with Flash without screwing it up again. He would be cool. He would be funny. He would impress her and to impress her was to impress himself because anyone who could impress Flash was impressive as hell.

He found her in his garage with her duffel bag over her shoulder.

"Thanks again for coming up here," he said as he unlocked the door to his house.

"No problem," she said. "I was thinking earlier today how much I wanted to drive to the top of a volcano covered in a foot of snow to do even more work."

"Two feet," he said. "We got dumped on two nights ago. Hope your truck has heating."

"It does. Although mine doesn't have fancy heated seats like somebody's does. You have a hot ass, Mr. Asher. Very hot…" As she walked past him into the house, she patted him on the seat of his pants, which were still warm from his new car's electric heated seats.

He took a moment to gently beat his head against the door frame before following her into the house.

He squared his shoulders and walked through the mud room into the living room. Flash stood in the center of the room, glancing around.

"Like it?" he asked.

"It's nice," she said. "I thought you said it was a fixer-upper. This all looks good. Is the knotty pine floor original?"

"It is," he said. "But I had to strip it and refinish it."

"You did it?"

"Yes," he said. "Believe it or not I am capable of doing some home improvement projects on my own. I do run a construction company, after all."

"You look supercute in your suit with your little hard hat on when you come to inspect us on-site."

"I wasn't always a suit," he said, throwing his coat and briefcase down on the kitchen counter. "I used to hang drywall and put down flooring. Let's see... I also poured concrete, painted, did a little basic masonry work and framed houses. I think I can strip and refinish a floor in my own house."

"I know," she said. "I just like giving you a hard time."

"Yeah, I've noticed."

"The floors look great with your dark green walls. Your paint job?"

"Yeah, thanks." He smiled hugely and then realized his "being cool" plan was already out the window if he was grinning like an idiot for the sole reason she'd complimented his wall color.

"Come here," he said. "I'll give you the ten-cent tour. The house was built in the 1940s. Three stories, cedar exterior, knotty pine floors. First floor is the living room and kitchen, second floor is the master bedroom, guest room and two bathrooms, top floor's the loft."

"What's in the loft?"

"Me," he said. "I sleep up there. Heat rises. Warmest room in the house at night. Plus it's the only room where you can see the top of the mountain in the morning. Very good view."

Ian paused, hoping she'd say something, anything, about wanting to see that view. But no, not a word.

"Um, all the furniture is made in Oregon," he said, pointing at the wood-framed couch, the rustic dining table and the cane-back rocking chair. "There's a hot tub outside."

"Oh, my."

"You like hot tubs?" he asked, a very pleasant image appearing unbidden in his mind, one that involved him and her and his hot tub and absolutely no clothing.

"Nope."

"Let me guess—you also hate puppies, kittens and chocolate."

"Yup."

"Liar," he said. She nodded, but that's all she did. No flirting, no teasing, no winking, no nothing.

"Okay, the fireplace is in the sitting room. Want to see it?"

"Please," she said. "That's why I'm here."

Luckily she was behind him and couldn't see him wince when she said that. All his hopes were fizzling like a wet firecracker. Why did he think he could make things right with her just by bringing her out to his house, getting her alone with him, hashing things out? Flash had already made her decision about him. If he were a gladiator and she the empress of Rome, she would have looked down on his beaten, bloodied and bruised body in the ring and given him a thumbs-down.

He led her through the living room to the rustic sitting room—oak bookcases, pine coffee table and his stone-and-iron fireplace, which was about to fall apart.

Ian pointed to a weak spot in the old irons screen.

"You can see that some of the joints are broken, and there's some rust." He grabbed a bar of the decorative iron grate and shook it so she could see how the central part of the design had come loose from the joints. "What do you think?"

Flash didn't say anything at first. She knelt onto the wood floor and ran her hands over the iron scrollwork.

"Ian…" she breathed. "It's beautiful."

He grinned again, like an idiot again, but this time he didn't chide himself for it.

"It's ivy," he said. "The whole thing is iron ivy. I thought you'd like it. It looks like the sort of thing you'd make."

"I would." Her eyes were alight with happiness and wonder as she ran her fingers all over the twisting and looping iron bars. "A real craftsman made this. Or craftswoman. This is art. Real folk art."

"It sold me on the house."

"It would have sold me, too," she said. "Wow."

"Oh, my God, did I hear Flash Redding say 'wow' to something? I never thought I'd live to see the day."

"I am not a hipster," she said. "I'm an artist with high standards. There's a difference. Hipsters pretend they aren't impressed by stuff. I'm genuinely not impressed by stuff. But this…this is wow. You done good. You have better eyes than I gave you credit for."

"I have a good eye for beauty," he said. She looked up at him and said nothing. But he could have sworn he saw a ghost of a smile dance across her lips before it disappeared into the hard line of her mouth again.

"I'll fix it," she said. "An artist needs to fix this, not just any welder. This is delicate work."

"Flash is on the job," he said. "Thank you."

"Flash again? Not Veronica?" she asked.

"You want me to call you Veronica?"

"No."

"Then I'll call you Flash. Why, I don't know. I assume you flashed someone at some point in the past and the name stuck?"

She shook her head in obvious disgust at his ignorance.

"Poor Ian. You've never seen *Flashdance*, have you?"

"*Flashdance?* The dance movie?"

"Yes, *Flashdance* is a dance movie."

"No, I haven't seen it. Why?"

"The main character in it is a woman who works as a welder by day and an exotic dancer by night. When I started welding in high school, one of my friends started calling me Flashdance. But I don't dance so it got shortened to Flash. I've been Flash ever since."

"Should I rent the movie?" They were having a good conversation. This was progress. This was an improvement. This was giving him hope.

"If you like to watch sexy girls dancing, maybe. And welding."

"I'm more into the welding than the dancing. I feel like I've missed out on something," he said as he knelt on the floor next to her and watched her test all the connections to see which ones were loose and needed to be rewelded. "Before my time, I guess."

"Before mine, too. But my mom did her job and showed me all her favorite movies when I was a kid."

"You have a mother?"

"Did you think I didn't?" she asked.

"Don't take it personally, I just assumed you were forged in the fires of Mordor."

She laughed softly. Yes…a laugh. Ten points for Asher.

"No, I have a mom. A cool mom. Everyone has a mom."

"I don't."

"Were you forged in the fires of Mordor?"

"I had a mom," he said. "But she died when I was a baby."

Flash looked at him and he looked away.

"I'm sorry. I didn't know. I'm an asshole."

"No, you aren't. You couldn't have known. She was hit by a drunk driver."

"Oh, my God, that's awful. I thought your parents were divorced. I didn't know your mom had been killed."

"They were separated when the accident happened. Dad's always felt bad about that. They'd eloped when she got pregnant with me and both families went to war. Her family hated him. His family hated her…"

"Romeo and Juliet."

"Sort of, yeah. If Romeo was Catholic and Juliet was Jewish."

"You're Jewish?"

"Mom was."

"Then you are, too. Judaism is passed through the

mother's line, not the father's. Mazel tov, Ian." She patted him on the head. He would have preferred a kiss but he'd take a head pat. At least she'd touched him.

"Are you Jewish?" he asked.

"I'm nothing," she said. "I just know about it because of a friend of mine."

"Boyfriend?"

"No, a friend-friend. You feel any different? Sudden craving for bagels? Suddenly annoyed at me for making a joke about Jewish people liking bagels?"

"I feel...I don't know how I feel," he said, trying to wrap his mind around this new information. It didn't make much of a dent on his soul, but still, it was good to know he had some sort of spiritual connection to his mother. "Dad never told me that. He never told me anything about Mom or that side of my family. He doesn't talk about her very much. Doesn't talk to her family. I've never even met my grandparents. Truth is, I think he was still in love with her and only separated because his family pressured him to and so did hers. He was only twenty and she was eighteen when they eloped."

"What was her name?"

He furrowed his brow. "You want to know my mother's name?"

"Yes, I want to know your mother's name. Why wouldn't I?"

He swallowed a sudden lump of sorrow. He didn't even remember his mother. Why would he be sad thirty-five years after she was gone?

Ian raised his hand and touched one of the iron leaves on the fireplace grate. "Riva," he said. "But when she went away to college, she went by Ivy. Dad said it was her teenage rebellion, changing her name. And marrying him."

"Rebellious teenager. I think I like your mom," she said.

He felt Flash's eyes boring into him, searching his face, studying him. What was she seeing?

"I can fix this," she said. "We can fix it. It'll be a lot of work, but we can fix it."

"The fireplace screen?"

"Yeah, the fireplace screen. What did you think I was talking about?"

"Nothing," he said. "I can pay you."

She stood up and looked down at him.

"I don't need your money," she said. "I'm not fixing this for you. I'm fixing it because it's beautiful and beautiful craftsmanship like this deserves being preserved by someone who knows what she's doing."

"Sorry," he said, standing up. "I wasn't trying to insult you. You said it was a big job. I don't want to take advantage of our…"

"What?"

"Friendship?"

"We aren't friends."

"Then what are we?" he asked.

"I don't know," she said. "But not friends."

She rubbed an iron vein on one of the iron stems of the ivy. A piece of rust flaked off on her finger and she shook her head at it like it had broken her heart.

"If we're not friends, then I should pay you," he said. "I'm not the sort of man who uses people. I'd have to fork over a thousand dollars to a pro to get this removed, cleaned, sanded, repaired and reinstalled. Either we're friends and you're helping me out of friendship, or you're a professional welder who is doing this as a job. So you either let me pay you to do the work or you admit we're friends."

"You can pay me," she said.

"Fine." It was anything but fine. He didn't mind paying her. But he wanted her to admit they were friends or something other than just employer-employee. She'd quit her job today and here she was again, working for him.

"In sex," she said.

"Excuse me?"

"You heard me." She wiped her hands on her pants. "You can pay me for the work in sex."

Ian blinked.

"You're not kidding."

"Why would I kid about that? You and I have already slept together. You know what I'm into. You're into it, too. And you're good at it, very good. It's not easy finding someone good in bed. That's valuable to me. I have money. I don't have someone to have good sex with. It's the barter system and don't pretend you don't want to. You could have asked Crawford to do this work for you. I'm not the only welder you know. I'm just the only welder you're attracted to."

"It's more than attraction," he said.

"What is it, then?"

"I don't know. But it's more."

"Whatever," she said with a shrug. "You decide."

"You are bizarre," he said.

"You're the one who started this so who's more bizarre—the girl with the blowtorch or the guy who wants to fuck the girl with the blowtorch?"

"The girl with the blowtorch. I'm going to go with that answer."

"Yeah, you're probably right about that."

"You don't even like me," he said, rubbing his temples in the hopes of keeping his brain from imploding. "You have made it abundantly clear you don't like me."

"I don't have to like someone to have good sex with them. I just have to respect them. You're a good boss, you run the company well, you treat your employees well and you don't take shortcuts with your work. That's attractive to me. I don't want to hold hands with you and go walking in a winter wonderland, but I'll spread for you if you're man enough to take me up on the offer. Because we both know you want to do it, and the only thing stopping you is fear."

"I'm not afraid."

"Yes, you are. You and I had an amazing night together and you dumped me because you were afraid of getting in trouble with dear old Senator Daddy."

"That's not why I dumped you."

"Then why?"

"Does it matter?" he asked.

"No skin off my rosy nose. So what'll it be? I can do this work in a day or two. Two days' work for two nights? What do you say?"

Ian wasn't prepared to answer that question because he hadn't been prepared to be asked that question. He'd been propositioned by a lot of women in his thirty-six years. Never once in those years had a woman attempted to barter welding services for sexual services. Was he flattered? A little. Was he insulted? Yeah. Kind of. A lot.

"No," he said. "That's what I say. No."

"Can I ask why you're saying no?"

"You can," he said.

She stared at him. He waited. She wasn't the only one who could play mind games.

"Why are you saying no?" she asked, her mouth a tight line of either tension or disappointment.

"I told you, I don't like using people. I don't like being used, either. I'm not going barter my body just so you can get off without getting attached. Thanks but no thanks. I'd rather sleep alone."

"Okay," she said. "That's fair." She pulled her phone out of her pocket and typed something. His own phone vibrated in his back pocket a second later.

"What did you send me?"

"The phone number of a guy named Daniel Tang. He's a metalsmith in Portland. He does killer work, and if you're willing to pay him to come out here, he will if you tell him my name." She zipped up her coat and glanced over her shoulder at the sky darkening through the picture window. "I better go. It's getting late."

She headed back toward the garage without another word.

Ian rubbed his temples again. This woman blew his mind on a daily basis. And she was leaving. Right now. He heard her in the living room picking up her gear from off the floor and heard her footsteps on the hardwood and heard the garage door opening. She was leaving and he was letting her go. He'd thought of her every single day and every single night for months. She intimidated him, she confused him, she intrigued him like no one else he'd ever met.

And he was letting her go.

No, he wasn't.

He ran through the house and made it to the door just in time to see her back out of his garage. She had her arm over the seat and was looking back as she turned around in his driveway. He waited and she looked his way one last time. He waved his arm to flag her down, to stop her, to slow her down, maybe. She gave him a little salute in return, and then drove out of his life.

She didn't even give him a chance to tell her goodbye.

3

FLASH CONGRATULATED HERSELF for not crying on the drive home to her apartment. She'd wanted to. She'd come very close. Then she'd seen that harrowing drop-off down the side of the highway and instead kept her eyes clear and on the road. By the time she pulled into her parking lot, she felt as good as anyone who'd been once again rejected by the guy she was in love with could feel.

"You don't love him," Flash told herself as she grabbed her duffel bag and a grocery bag from behind her truck seat. "You just want him."

She closed her eyes and breathed long and hard through her nose, willing herself not to love Ian. A long time ago she'd read about those gurus who could control their own heart rates, slowing them to the point people could mistake them for dead. Why couldn't she do that? She should be able to do that, will her heart to not beat so wildly in Ian's presence. When he'd said his mother's name and touched the iron ivy leaf on the fireplace grate, she thought she'd die of love for the man. If he was just a pretty face with good hair and a great body and a nice smile, and even if he was just a good person, she might have made it out without falling in love with him. But he was all that and vulnerable, too. That was her Achilles' heel, her Kryptonite, the one chink in the armor she'd forged for herself. She felt protective of him as she never felt about any other man. She wanted to take care of him, which was stupid because if anyone on earth didn't need taking care of it was the son of a rich father with a good job and all the luxuries in his life money could buy. But still…it was there, that love, that need to take care of him, and when he'd said he refused to let her use him, she'd almost broken down right then and told him everything she felt about him including all of that. Instead she'd turned tail and ran. He'd offered her friendship when she wanted his body and his heart and his soul. Friendship was the last thing she wanted from Ian Asher.

With a sigh, she got out of her truck, took her bags and walked to the corner apartment on the first floor. A few people had already started decorating for Christmas. She saw lights in windows, battery-operated candles, a few fake snow scenes. Fake snow? All they had to do was drive thirty miles east and they'd be up to their eyebrows in real snow.

She doubled-checked her grocery bag out of paranoia and knocked on the one door on the row with no Christmas decorations in the windows.

A few seconds later the door opened a crack, the security chain still locked.

"You're late," the voice inside the door said.

"Work-related. Sorry."

"You have the stuff?"

"I have it," Flash said.

"Two bags?"

"Two bags."

"Anybody see you come here?" the voice asked, and Flash saw two dark brown eyes darting around in the direction of the parking lot.

"Nobody saw me but someone's going to if you don't let me in."

The door slammed shut and a second later reopened. Flash slipped inside.

"You know this stuff isn't illegal, right?" Flash said, passing the grocery bag to her downstairs neighbor, Mrs. Leah Scheinberg.

"Illegal or not, I can't get caught with it," Mrs. Scheinberg said, digging through the bag with a grin on her face. "I'd never hear the end of it. Here, take a hit. You look like you need this as much as I do."

Mrs. Scheinberg was eighty-eight years old and had spent World War II working in a munitions factory as a welder—a real live Rosie the Riveter. Flash worshiped the ground she walked on, especially since Mrs. Scheinberg had saved one of her blowtorches from back in the day and had given it to her. Now it was Flash's most prized possession. So when Mrs. Scheinberg offered her a frosted Christmas cookie, Flash took it, because when a woman is as much of a badass at eighty-eight as she was at eighteen, you ate the cookies she gave you and you did it with a smile.

"These are pretty good," Flash said, eating an iced Christmas tree in one bite. "No wonder you make me smuggle them to you."

"If my son weren't such a stick-in-the-mud, I wouldn't have to have you smuggle them in for me. Sit," Mrs. Scheinberg said, pointing at her sofa.

Flash sat and munched on the fistful of cookies she'd

taken out of the bag. She loved hanging out at Mrs. Scheinberg's apartment. It was like stepping back in time to the 1930s. She'd inherited all her parents' furniture and had it cleaned and repaired so that it looked like new, even if the patterns and styles were from another era. She had art deco lamps on her side tables with geometric patterned shades, a square teak coffee table with chrome legs and a leopard print wall-hanging over the back of the two-tone black-and-white sofa. Mrs. Scheinberg herself looked like she belonged in another era. She wore dresses every single day—not skirts, but dresses. When she went out she put on gloves. When she stayed in she always had on a full face of makeup and had her white hair styled every week. She took a seat in the chair across from the sofa and crossed her legs at the ankles, prim as a schoolgirl while she scarfed down frosted Christmas cookies like a starving person.

"Talk," Mrs. Scheinberg said between bites. "Why were you late? You put in your notice today?"

"I did."

"How did Mr. Asher take it?" Mrs. Scheinberg paused in her munching long enough to give Flash a pointed look.

"He took it. He wasn't happy about it but he said he understood."

Mrs. Scheinberg waved her hand dismissively.

"Not good enough for you," Mrs. Scheinberg said. "You're better off without him."

"I did find something out about him today, though," Flash said. "Something surprising."

"Spill it," Mrs. Scheinberg said, then popped another cookie in her mouth.

"He's Jewish."

Mrs. Scheinberg nodded her approval. "I always liked the boy."

"You just told me he wasn't good enough for me."

"That's before you told me he was a nice Jewish boy. Why am I just hearing this?"

"Because he didn't know. We were talking about our parents and he mentioned that his mom died when he was a baby. He said his father never talks about her because there's a lot of bad blood between the two sides of the family. His dad's Catholic and his mother was from a pretty conservative Jewish family apparently."

"Then he's Jewish."

"That's what I told him. Then I asked him if he wanted a bagel."

"Wicked girl. In my day we didn't talk to men like that. Well...I did. But most women didn't."

"I can't help myself," Flash said. "He's infuriating. I can't stand being around him. I want to insult him and yell at him and put a 'kick me' sign on his back. He turns me into a child. I'm twenty-six. I should be able to talk to a man I'm attracted to without insulting him."

"You're in love."

"Yup."

"And you're scared."

"Yup."

"Sit up straight and talk to me like a grown woman, Veronica Redding. We're adults here. Let's act like them." She snapped her fingers and Flash sighed and sat up straighter.

"You don't have much room to talk," Flash said. "You're Jewish but you're addicted to frosted Christmas cookies and you make me buy them for you so your son won't find out."

"Where did I go wrong with that boy?"

"Your son runs an entire hospital. He calls you every day. He checks on you three times a week. And he's nice to me. Nobody's nice to me but he's nice to me."

"Yes, but he has no sense of humor. My son should have a sense of humor. If he caught me with these, he'd throw them in the trash and tell me I shouldn't be eating goyische food."

"That's terrible. If he catches you with them, tell him they're mine and you were just holding them for me."

Mrs. Scheinberg laughed. "He'd see right through it."

"Fine, I'll keep smuggling them to you. As long as you share."

"I always share with my girl," Mrs. Scheinberg said, leaning forward to pat Flash on the knee. "Now tell me more about Mr. Asher. Why were you two talking about mothers?"

"I don't even remember how we got on the topic. I put in my notice and said goodbye. I was already to the truck when he came out and asked me to stop by his new house and help him with a project. He's got this fireplace thing that needs some major repairs and it's…wow. It's a work of art. But it's rusted and broken."

"It needs your help."

"It does."

"So you're going help Mr. Asher?"

"No."

"You told him no? Are you that angry at the man?"

"I'm not angry at him. I'm not. Not really. Not much, anyway."

Mrs. Scheinberg raised her eyebrow.

"Okay, I'm angry at him," Flash said. "He dumped me."

"You work for him. You expect too much of a man

when you ask him to compromise his integrity so you can have a boyfriend."

"He shouldn't have slept with me if he felt that way."

"No, he shouldn't have. But you were there, too. Don't act like you were some kind of victim. We both know you were after him even before that night."

Flash smiled. "I was after him. You would be, too, if you saw him."

"Oh, I've seen him."

"You've seen him?"

"I Googled him. Handsome, very handsome. Nice face, nice hair and nice eyes. Big shoulders. Good strong neck. I loved Dr. Scheinberg's neck. I liked to nibble it at stoplights in the car. He'd drive home a little faster when I did."

"Mrs. Scheinberg!"

She waved her hand again, poo-pooing Flash's shock.

"Don't be silly. We were married. Sex between a husband and a wife is a mitzvah. And, oh, was it a mitzvah with him."

"I should do a mitzvah for Ian. I was…not nice to him."

Mrs. Scheinberg had explained mitzvot were something like commandments. But more than that, more like good deeds or blessings.

"What happened?" Mrs. Scheinberg asked. "And do I want to know?"

"He offered me his friendship and I said no way. He offered to pay me for helping him fix his fireplace screen, and I said I'd do it if he slept with me."

"Young lady, that is shameful."

"I know, I know." Flash buried her head in her hands before looking up again. "He's never going to love me.

Men like that don't love women like me. They screw women like me. They don't marry women like me and make me part of their perfect prissy lives."

"Women like you? What's a woman like you?"

"I'm blue collar. Ian is very white collar. Seriously, he has the whitest collars I've ever seen. He must own stock in a bleach company."

"I was a welder, too, and I married a doctor."

"You were a teenage welder because you were helping with the war effort."

"My mother was a housewife and my father a baker. We were poor, dear. And Dr. Scheinberg was anything but. Now stop with the inferiority complex. Any man would be lucky to have you. Including Mr. Ian Asher. Especially Mr. Ian Asher. And I think he knows it already, which is why he offered his friendship."

Mrs. Scheinberg stood up and wiped her hands on a lacy handkerchief that Flash guessed had belonged to her mother, much like everything else in this room.

"I think he's afraid of me."

"I can't imagine why," Mrs. Scheinberg said over her shoulder as she walked to her dining room table. "It isn't like you've purposely tried to terrorize him by playing schoolyard pranks on him."

"I'm not very good at relationships."

"You'll get better with practice."

"What should I do?"

"I think you should apologize to him for trying to buy his body."

"But it's such a nice body." Flash sighed. "Do you think I should try being friends with him?"

"Being just friends with someone you're in love with can be hard. And dishonest if you're only using the friendship in the hopes of it becoming something more." Mrs. Scheinberg took the lid of a blue-and-white box on her table and removed something from the box wrapped in blue velvet.

"What's that?"

"My Hanukkiah, but you'd call it a menorah, my darling gentile," Mrs. Scheinberg said as she carefully unwrapped a silver nine-branched candelabrum. "Moshe gave it to me after he and his wife came back from their last trip to Israel. Isn't it beautiful?"

Flash walked over to the table and sat down, studying the menorah. It was beautiful. She touched the base—real silver.

"When does Hanukkah start?" she asked.

"Tomorrow evening. Moshe and Hannah are coming over. And Tova, too. If you can behave yourself for one evening, you can come. We'd love to have you."

Flash gave Mrs. Scheinberg a skeptical look.

"Well, I'd love to have you," Mrs. Scheinberg said. "Hannah thinks you're a little strange. I said you're not strange. You're a BMW. I didn't tell her what that meant."

Flash laughed. BMW stood for Burly Mountain Woman, which is what the tough ladies who lived on Mount Hood often called themselves.

"Can you fetch me the silver polish? It's under the sink."

Flash found the polish but before leaving Mrs. Scheinberg's kitchen she paused and studied the photographs on the refrigerator. They were all of Mrs. Scheinberg with her family—her two sons, her seven grandchildren, an old black-and-white photo of her and her husband, Dr. Lawrence Scheinberg, who'd been

movie-star handsome in his prime, a young Humphrey
Bogart with thick wavy hair. One photograph was from
last year, all the family gathered around a table with
Mrs. Scheinberg's silver menorah front and center. Mrs.
Scheinberg had been lighting the very last candle when
the photograph had been taken. Everyone in the picture wore a beautiful smile, the same smile, the smile
of family. Flash felt a pang of sympathy for Ian. He'd
never gotten to take a family photograph like this with
his mother and grandparents and cousins. He'd never
had the chance to celebrate the holidays that were part
of his heritage, never a chance to light a candle on a
menorah.

"Mrs. Scheinberg?"

"Yes, dear?"

"Are there rules about menorahs? I mean, Hanuk-
kiahs?"

"Rules? What do you mean?"

She brought Mrs. Scheinberg the silver polish and
a chamois.

"Rules about how they have to be made? Or blessed?"

"It should have nine branches, nine candle holders or
nine oil holders. Usually eight are in a line. The ninth
has to be higher than the other eight."

"That's it?"

"They should be made well. That's all I can think of.
Why do you ask?"

Flash opened the bottle of cleaner and went to work
polishing the menorah for Mrs. Scheinberg. She had ar-
thritis in her hands and Flash knew it pained her.

"I have an idea for a mitzvah to do for Ian."

4

IAN SPENT ALL day working on the new house and trying not to think about Flash. He stripped the old paper out of the downstairs bathroom, sanded the drywall and repainted it the same deep forest green as the living room walls. A huge job for one man and it took him from seven in the morning until five that evening to finish the work. By dinnertime, he was sore, tired and covered in paint and wall dust. He was hungry, too, but couldn't bring himself to eat until he'd cleaned up. He stood under the hot water in the shower for as long as he could stand the heat. He'd hoped the hard work would distract him from thinking about Flash but it didn't, not even close. She'd been on his mind from sunrise until sunset, and if tonight were anything like last night, she'd be on his mind until dawn. Why couldn't he just forget about her? She didn't like him. She only liked having sex with him. He wanted more than that. She didn't. She didn't even want to be friends with him. Maybe she was smart to turn down his offer of friendship. Likely she saw right through it and knew he wanted more than she was willing to give him. Or she knew he was desperate to get closer to her and she simply liked to torture him.

Reluctantly he turned off the shower when the hot water started to run out. He toweled off, pulled on his jeans, ran his fingers through his hair, and walked out of the bathroom.

"Goddamn, you take long showers," Flash said. Ian stared into the master bedroom where Flash Redding sat in a leather armchair. He didn't see all of her because the back of the chair faced the bathroom door. It hadn't before he'd gotten into the shower but she must have turned it around while he was in the bathroom. He saw her legs dangling over the chair arm and her beat-up red Pumas dangling off her feet. Of course she wore Pumas. Nike owned one half of Portland and Adidas owned the other half. Even her sneakers were subversive.

"Flash, what the fuck are you doing in my house?"

"You invited me over."

"Yesterday. I invited you over *yesterday*. And you came over yesterday. And then you left. That wasn't an open invitation to come into my house anytime you wanted."

"Should I leave?"

"I don't know. Tell me why you're here, and I'll tell you if you should leave or not."

"Are you decent?"

"I have jeans on."

"Bummer."

"You were trying to catch me naked?" he asked as he walked over and tossed his towel in the laundry hamper. She wore burgundy skinny jeans and a white sleeveless undershirt, which she called a "wifebeater" no matter how many times he told her she shouldn't use that term. Her brown bomber jacket hung off the bedpost knob.

"No, but I wouldn't have complained if you were."

"You know this is creepy, right? You coming into my house while I'm in the shower?" He hated how much he liked seeing her making herself at home in his place. Especially since she was technically breaking and entering.

"Is it?"

"Let's do a little role reversal here. You're in the shower—"

She started to take her shirt off.

"Not actually in the shower," he said.

"Fine. Go on." She lowered her arms.

"You're in the shower at your place and you walk out of the shower and I'm in your living room. How does that make you feel?" Ian asked.

"I don't know," Flash said. "Why are you in my living room in this scenario?"

"It doesn't matter."

"It does matter. If you're in my living room to rob me, I'd be pissed. If you were in my living room to surprise me with red velvet cupcakes, I'd be happy. If you were in my living room because you're running from killer ninjas, then I would be surprised because I'm not entirely sure ninjas exist, and if they do, I highly doubt you'd get mixed up in anything that would make ninjas want to kill you. But I wouldn't be mad. I'd be impressed you got away from them. And then I would go join up with them because I've always wanted to be a ninja," Flash said.

"Flash."

"Yes?"

"Why are you in my house?"

"I have a gift for you."

If she'd said she was in his house to assassinate him because she herself was a ninja and had been given orders to kill him, he would have been less surprised than he was at that moment when Flash Redding, a woman he was dead certain loathed him, said she had a gift for him.

"It's not a throwing star, is it?"

"No, but I could make one if you want one. I've never made one before, though. That's a lie. I have made them. I've made lots of them."

"Flash."

"What?"

"You're behaving very strangely."

"How am I behaving?"

"You're being...adorable," he said. "And kind of nice. It's freaking me out."

"Imagine how I feel."

He pulled a plain black T-shirt out of his clean laundry basket and pulled it on. This was not a conversation he should be having half-dressed. He needed to be fully dressed and probably a bulletproof vest wouldn't hurt, either.

"What are you doing here, Veronica?" he asked, hoping if he used her real name he'd get the real person to talk.

"You wanted to be friends with me and I said no. I changed my mind. I have some friends who feel comfortable coming over to my place and making themselves at home. I thought it was what close friends did. I'm sorry. I didn't mean to freak you out. It's twenty-two degrees out and you didn't answer the door when

I knocked even though I know you're here because I saw your car in the garage window. I came in instead of freezing to death in my truck. I heard you in the shower so I waited outside not facing the shower in case you walk around in the buff like I do."

"Okay," he said. "That's a semireasonable statement. I have some friends who'd do the same thing. So...we're friends now?"

"Maybe. I don't know. Probably not, but I wanted to give you something, anyway, as an apology for my bad behavior the past few months. You know, the thing with the truck nuts and what not. So here." She picked up a box that she'd set on the floor by the leather chair and thrust it into his hands. Then she picked up her jacket and started to leave the room.

"Wait. Where are you going?"

"I gave you the thing," she said.

"You aren't going to stay and watch me open it?"

"Is that something you're into?" she asked.

"I...guess? I think so? Plus if it's a bomb I want to make sure you get hit, too."

"Good idea. But it's not a bomb."

"What is it?"

"Open it," she said.

"Fine. I'm opening it." He sat down in the chair and ripped the brown paper off the box and opened the lid. There was something wrapped in white tissue paper inside. Too big to be a throwing star. Too small to be a bomb. Unless it was a very small bomb.

Carefully he peeled back the tissue paper.

"It's a candleholder," he said, taking it out of the box.

"It's a Hanukkiah," she said.

"A what?"

"It's like a menorah. You light the candles to celebrate Hanukkah. So... Happy Hanukkah."

"I found out I was Jewish yesterday."

"And today's the first day of Hanukkah. I made it. The branches are ivy, see?"

She pointed at the eight branches that looked like normal candle arms until one looked closely and saw they were small and twisting vines of ivy.

"You made this?"

"Last night and today," she said. "I didn't have anything else to do. Wait. That's mean. I had a lot to do, but I did that instead because it was important to me to give you a gift that was meaningful and took work. And it took a lot of work. Not a ton, because I'm good, but a lot. I hope you like it. I think it's pretty."

"It's...wow. It's beautiful."

"I made it ivy because of your mom. I thought you should have something to connect you to her. My mom and I are really close. It's awful you never got to know yours."

Ian took a long breath and used the menorah to avoid looking at Flash. It was a work of art, this menorah. He didn't know anything about them, how to use them, what they meant, but he knew it was special and that he was grateful to have it.

"Thank you," he said, looking up at her at last.

"There are candles in the bottom of the box. Mrs. Scheinberg said you can only use the candles for the menorah. It's part of the ritual. If you want to talk to her about Judaism or anything, she said you can call her or come visit. She's supernice."

"Who's Mrs. Scheinberg?"

"She's my eighty-eight-year-old downstairs neighbor. She's Jewish. She's also my best friend."

"You have an eighty-eight-year-old best friend?"

She nodded.

"You don't do anything the normal way, do you?" he asked.

"Normal is boring. And Mrs. Scheinberg is the shit. She was a welder during the war. She was even in a pinup calendar that was sent to the troops, can you believe it? I saw the picture. Betty Grable had nothing on this lady's gams."

Flash spoke quickly, a flood of words tumbling from her mouth. She seemed...nervous. Being friendly was clearly hard for her. It was insanely endearing seeing her nervous.

"Do you want to light the candles?" she asked. "It's sunset. Mrs. Scheinberg said that's when you light the first candle."

"I don't have a—"

She whipped a lighter out of her pocket, and flicked the flame on before he could finish the sentence.

"Okay, so you have a lighter."

"Never know when you're gonna need one," she said. "Where should we put it?"

"In the window, I guess," Ian said, embarrassingly happy that she used the word *we*.

"Which window?" Flash turned around. There were two large windows in the master bedroom.

"Upstairs," he said.

"But this is the master bedroom, isn't it?" she asked, following him up the stairs with the box full of candles.

"Guest room. I like to sleep up here," he said as he headed to the spiral staircase that led from the hallway up to the third-floor loft. The third floor of an A-frame house was the smallest and narrowest. There wasn't much room except for his bed and a few feet on either side of it. But he liked how high up he was here and how far he could see from the top window. He set the menorah into the bedroom window and sat at the end of his bed.

"How do we do this?" he asked.

"Don't know, I'm not Jewish. You are."

"Great. I've been Jewish for one day and I'm already failing at it," he said.

"Hold on." She pulled her phone from her pants pocket and typed something in. "Okay, Google says to put a candle into the far right candleholder and then light the Shamash."

"What's a Shamash?"

"It's the candle that's used to light the other candles, it says. You only use that candle. Never use one menorah candle to light the other candles. So the Shamash goes here." She pointed at the center candleholder that was two inches higher than the others. "Got it?"

"I think so. God forgive me if I do this wrong."

"I imagine he's pretty forgiving with noobs."

"Is that what God calls us? Noobs?"

"Well, whatever the Hebrew word for 'newbie' is. I'll ask Mrs. Scheinberg next time I see her. Oh, there's some blessings you're supposed to say."

"What are they?" Ian asked, feeling wildly uncomfortable with the thought of reciting blessings. He rarely even attended Mass these days.

"I don't know. They're all in Hebrew. I can Google—"

"We'll skip it. I'm a newbie, remember." He took the lighter from her hand and lit the one candle that went into the center. Then he used it to light the candle on the far right. "Sorry I'm such a noob, God. You know what I'm supposed to say better than I do."

"Sounds like a good prayer to me," she said. She sat on the bed next to him and side by side they stared at the burning lights. "It's pretty."

"Beautiful."

"I'm glad you like it. I wanted you to like it."

"It means a lot to me that you did this," he said. "I know we've hurt each other in the past. I've hurt you."

"I wish you hadn't dumped me—or at least not dumped me like you did—but Mrs. Scheinberg said you did it out of your integrity and I shouldn't blame you."

"Flash...here's the thing," he began. "The night we spent together was incredible."

"Hell, yeah, it was."

"So incredible that I was going to go talk to Dad and explain the situation—that I was romantically interested in someone who worked for the company, and I wanted to see how to handle it. You know, transfer to another job or something. But before I could go talk to him, something happened."

Ian didn't know how to say the next part. He didn't want to. He hated to embarrass her but he had to tell her. She had to know.

"You remember a guy named John Haggerty?" Ian asked.

"Yeah, drywall guy. He asked me out like five times before I told him I was going to report him if he talked to me again."

"When I came into work the morning after that night, Haggerty was sitting in front of my desk, waiting for me. He said he had something to tell me. He said it was about us."

Flash's eyes widened. He went on before she could ask.

"That night at the bar in Portland, we left together. You remember that?"

She nodded.

"And you remember I kissed you while we were leaving the bar?"

She nodded again.

"And you remember the bar was kind of dark by that time?"

She nodded once more.

"Haggerty was in the bar," Ian said. "Not only did he see us alone together drinking and flirting. He saw us kissing. He saw us leave together. And he took pictures of it all."

"Ah…" She closed her eyes and exhaled.

"Haggerty said he wanted a ten thousand dollar 'bonus' or he would tape those pictures inside every single locker at the company. He'd also send them to the news so they'd know that Oregon State Senator Dean Asher's son likes to fuck his female employees, and all of this happens on my father's watch and wouldn't that make a great headline. Haggerty's a piece of shit but he's a smart piece of shit. He knew how much trouble he could cause with a potential sexual harassment scandal. He was so smug sitting there I wanted to smash his face in. I almost did it, too."

"What did you do?"

"I told him I had to see how I could do this without Dad catching on. He said I had twenty-four hours before he told everyone about us and started pasting up pictures. Soon as he left the office, I called the company lawyer."

"So you dumped me because you didn't want your dad getting in trouble?"

"I broke it off with you because our lawyer said I needed to. He said you were a ticking time bomb, the only woman who worked on the construction crew, and I'd slept with you. If it made the news or you decided to sue or something…"

Flash made a sound like a bomb going off.

"Yeah," Ian said. "Our lawyer was ready to kill me. Dad's a state senator, he said like I didn't know that already. Lawsuits. Cover-ups. Do not piss off the unions during an election year. Hell hath no fury like a woman scorned and on and on about how precarious the situation was. That's the word he used—*precarious*."

"Good word."

"He said I had a choice—either I had to break it off with you completely and forever or I had to tell Dad and let Dad fire you."

"Fire me?"

"You'd played a couple small pranks on coworkers and the lawyer said those constitute more than enough legal grounds to fire you."

"We all play pranks on each other. Nobody ever gets hurt."

"I know, I know." Ian raised his hands in surrender. "That's what I told Mac Brand, the company shark. He said I had to decide—either I dump you or fire you. It was so unfair to you in every single way but I didn't see any other choice. I told our lawyer I'd break it off with you. He called the police and the next morning when Haggerty came into my office, I recorded our conversation, and got him arrested for blackmail. We agreed to drop the charges if he signed a legally binding nondisclosure agreement. And that was the end of it. And us."

Ian felt sick, physically ill, recounting the story to her. He'd wanted to spare her the details, protect her from the knowledge of what could have been a nightmare for her.

"That's very sweet, Ian. But…"

"But?"

"But you should have talked to me. You should have told me what was really going on instead of saying, 'Sorry, sweetheart. You're not good enough for me.'"

"That's not what I said. I said I'm your 'superior' because I am literally your 'superior.' That's the word they use for a boss who oversees your work. Your 'superior.' I had the company lawyer telling me to find a reason to fire you, and I could have done it and you wouldn't have had a legal leg to stand on. That's too much power to have over the person you're dating. I'm sorry I didn't tell you the whole truth. I wanted to protect you. That's all. There's my confession. Not a week goes by I don't tell myself I made the wrong decision, although for the life of me, I don't know what other choice I had."

"You could have told me what was happening. You could have told me the entire truth. You could have mentioned to me that someone was blackmailing you and threatening to ruin your dad's political career. I would have been upset, but I also would have been sympathetic. And I would have handled it my own way without getting lawyers involved."

"What would you have done? Or do I not want to know?"

"I would have told everyone at work you and I slept together."

"That's how you would have handled it?"

"You can only blackmail someone over a secret. If it's not a secret, then they can't blackmail you, right?"

"True. Then again if you went around telling everyone at work about your sex life, you could have been fired for creating a hostile work environment."

"What? Are you serious?"

"Now you see what an untenable position I was in?" he asked. "There was no way to win for you or me or us, only better ways of losing. Like could I let them fire you when you'd done nothing wrong so we could cover our asses? Not a chance."

"Wow." It was all Flash said and then she said nothing more for a long time. He looked at the menorah she'd made him and saw it for what it was—a peace offering. He wished he had something more to give her in return than an ugly story.

"I know I was cold when I broke it off with you," Ian said. "I know I was an ass. I know I was being insulting by telling you I was your superior."

"You said, 'Someone like me can't be involved with someone like you,'" she said.

"I meant a boss with an employee. That's all."

"I thought you meant…"

"You thought I meant you weren't good enough for me," he said. "That's not what I meant. It's not what I meant because it's not what I think or what I feel. I wanted to talk to you about it, you know, after all the dust settled. But you'd already moved on and put it behind you. At least it seemed like you did."

"Yeah, well, Mom and I moved a ton when I was a

kid. She'd get behind on the rent and we'd have to pack up the car and drive out in the middle of the night, start over somewhere new a week later. At first you come to a new town and try to make friends. Then you move and lose your friends. By the fifth and sixth town you know you're going to move again so you might as well not make friends. I got very good at walking away and leaving people behind. It was a survival skill. I had to learn fast how to cut my losses. Rule number one— don't get attached in the first place and then when you leave you won't miss anything. Or anybody. I broke rule number one with you. I got attached. But I didn't break rule number two."

"What's rule number two?"

"When you see that you're losing, quit playing. I was losing you so I folded my cards and left the table. I don't stay where I'm not wanted."

"You were wanted," Ian whispered.

She stood up but immediately sat down again, not on the bed but on the floor with her back to the wall and the menorah in the window to her right. The candlelight danced across her face. She'd never looked more lovely to him or young or small or vulnerable. In personality and presence, she was huge. Physically she was a shrimp. An incredibly sexy shrimp.

"If I'd known you still wanted me…" she said, and paused.

"What would you have done?"

"I would have quit my job," she said. "So we could have kept seeing each other without you getting into trouble or your dad. Or me."

"You did quit your job."

"Too late," she said.

"Flash, you know I'm sorry, right? About everything?"

And he was sorry. After he broke it off with Flash he'd determined to put the whole thing behind him. He'd let his father set him up on blind dates with preapproved women, mostly the daughters of friends and business colleagues. Ian had done it; he'd gone out with his father's choices. Every last woman he went out with on these father-ordained blind dates had been elegant, sophisticated, with long hair, understated makeup, no tattoos and no piercings other than the earlobes. They were all in respectable lines of work—one professor at a Catholic college, one doctor of internal medicine, one financial lawyer who sat on the board of one of Dad's favorite charities. All wonderful women—smart, attractive and accomplished. When his father demanded to know why Ian hadn't asked any of them out on a second date, all Ian had said was, *Sorry, she's just not my type*, when what he meant was, *I'm not over Flash and I don't know if I ever will be.*

"I regret it," Ian said when Flash didn't say anything to his apology. "And I'm not proud of myself. As much as my father loves me and I love him, there was a damn good chance he'd fire me if he found out what was going on. I'd not only slept with an employee, but I'd gotten caught sleeping with an employee. I didn't want you to lose your job. I didn't want me to lose my father's respect." Ian rubbed his face and groaned before dropping his hands to his knees and meeting her eyes again. "I made the wrong choice by not telling you the truth. It was a weak thing to do and I don't like thinking of myself as a weak man. I wanted to beat Haggerty for threatening to do that to me, to us. Literally physically beat the shit out of him so much it scared me. I scared me. My feelings scared me. So I…" He shrugged.

"You cut your losses."

"That's what I thought I was doing," he said. "Cutting my losses. I lost too much when I lost you. And when you quit work and walked out of the building, it felt like I was about to lose something I couldn't live without."

"Dammit, Ian, I wish you'd told me all of this back then instead of keeping it from me," she said.

"I do, too," he said. "Can you forgive me?"

It felt like an eternity passed before she finally answered him.

"Yeah, I can forgive you."

"I don't deserve it. You're a better person than I am."

"I know," she said, the tiniest hint of a smile on her mouth.

"I want to be with you," he said. "In any way you'll let me be with you. If you want to have sex—just sex—I can live with that. It's not what I want but if it makes you happy, if it makes up for what I did, I'll do it."

"What do you want from me? And don't say you want to be my friend. We both know that's not it."

"I want you. As much of you as you are willing to give me. I can't deal with watching you walk out of my life again. You did it yesterday and I lasted three seconds before I was chasing you across the parking lot. You did it last night and I lasted two seconds before I was running to the garage to stop you. I screwed up last time. I'm not going to screw up this time. Please tell me you'll give me another chance, Flash. That's all I'm asking for."

"I'm here," she said. "I drove to the top of a volcano that's covered in two feet of snow to give you a gift

I made with my own hands today. Did I mention the volcano part?" She turned to point at the top of Mount Hood, its snowy peak glowing a red and sunset gold in the window.

"The volcano thing makes you nervous, doesn't it?"

"You make me nervous," she said, turning away from the window to meet his eyes.

"I make you nervous? Me? Ian Asher makes Flash Redding nervous? That's like saying David made Goliath nervous."

"David killed Goliath," she said.

"But David didn't make Goliath nervous."

"If Goliath were smart, he would have been nervous," she said. "I'm smart enough to be nervous."

She raised her chin and looked him hard in the eyes, daring him to take this where he knew they both wanted it to go.

"Tell me why I make you nervous," he said. The time for questions was over. Orders only.

"Because I have very strong feelings for you," she said.

"I have strong feelings for you, too."

"Anger? Fear? The usual dark-side stuff?" she asked.

"Attraction, fascination, adoration, affection, erection."

"Is 'erection' an emotion?" she asked.

"It's definitely a feeling."

"What's it feel like?" she asked, walking right into his answer, which he knew she did on purpose, because she wanted this as much as he did.

"Come here and find out for yourself."

5

FLASH GAVE HIM a long look and didn't speak. They were in a standoff and he'd just fired the first shot. Now it was her move.

She started to stand and Ian shook his head.

"You know better than that," he said.

Flash lowered herself back to the floor. She didn't move again, not for a few seconds. Stubborn girl, he knew she wanted it as much as he did. And she knew he knew, which was why she took her own sweet time obeying him.

Not that he minded. He could wait. Luckily he didn't have to wait long. Flash slowly tipped forward and came up onto her hands and knees. She crawled four feet from the wall to the end of his bed. Every muscle in his body went taut at the sight of this invincible woman on her knees in front of him. His chest heaved as she knelt between his thighs and his blood rushed and burned. She hadn't even touched him yet.

This time he made her wait, made her sit there while he took her chin in his hand and turned her face left and right and then finally up to meet his eyes.

"So beautiful," he said. "I like the nose stud." He tapped the end of her nose to make her smile.

"Thank you," she said. No sarcasm. No talking back. She laid her head on his thigh and he couldn't help but feel that was exactly where it belonged.

"I love the way your hair looks after you take your welding helmet off. Sometimes you spike your hair up on purpose. But that's when it's spiked up just because it's sweaty and out of control. It looks like you've just been fucked, long and hard. I like that image in my head."

"Me being fucked long and hard?"

"Me. Fucking you. Long and hard," he said.

"I like that image, too."

With his hand still on her chin, he traced the outline of her lips with his thumb. She had full soft kissable lips, the kind of lips a man dreams of seeing wrapped around his cock morning, noon and night. Their first and only night together he'd made her suck him off the second they were inside the door of his Pearl District apartment. He'd been leaning back against his own front door, his hands twisted in her hair, and his cock down her throat. And the entire city of Portland lay before him outside his sky rise window that looked down onto the Columbia River. It felt like they were putting on a show for the town. They'd made it a damn good show.

Ian pushed his thumb past her lips and into her mouth, resting the pad on top of her tongue.

"I remember this mouth," he said softly. "I remember how it felt on my cock. I remember this tongue licking me. You wanted it even more than I did. I didn't even have to tell you twice to get on your knees. I kissed you, whispered, 'Suck me off,' in your ear and you hit your knees so fast I thought you saw someone with a gun outside the window."

She couldn't laugh with his thumb in her mouth holding her tongue down, but he felt her body shiver with the suppressed chuckle.

"You moaned when I put my hand on the back of your head," he said, lightly fucking her mouth now with his thumb. "I'd never had a woman moan with pleasure while she was going down on me. But you did. That's when I knew you and I would get along just fine... wouldn't we?"

She closed her eyes and nodded. Her dark lashes, heavy and thick with black mascara and eyeliner, fluttered on her cheeks. The softest moan escaped the back of her throat.

"You want me," Ian said. "You want my cock."

She nodded again, eyes still closed. He stroked her tongue again with the pad of his thumb. Soft and wet and warm, he needed that tongue on his body.

"Suck me," he said. "But don't make me come yet. I'm saving that for later."

He pulled his thumb from her mouth and leaned back on the bed on his hands. Flash didn't hesitate one second, not that he expected her to. She unbuttoned his jeans with eager, dexterous fingers, pulled the zipper down carefully and lifted his T-shirt to press a long hot kiss onto his lower stomach. Ian wrapped his feet around her thighs to trap her body between his legs.

Ian didn't allow himself to make any sounds when she put his cock into her mouth. He'd make her work for it before he rewarded her. Oh, but he could have groaned when she sucked him deep into her hot mouth. He'd thought of this a thousand times since their one night together. He'd dreamed about it and woken up hard. He'd even come in his sleep once while dreaming about Flash sucking his cock, something he hadn't done since he was a teenage boy. He dug his fingers deep into the sheets of his bed to keep himself from coming immediately into her mouth. For six months he'd ached to have this again. Six months was a very long time to go between the two sexiest blow jobs of his life.

Flash touched him while she sucked him like she did last time. She seemed particularly fond of his stomach and the bottom of his rib cage, which she tickled and traced with her fingertips. She loved his body and he knew it because she'd told him that night not only in words but with her every hungry touch. He'd held her down onto the bed by her wrists and she'd pouted because she couldn't touch him like that. Eight thick inches of cock inside her and still she'd wanted more of him. He'd laughed and called her greedy. She'd said, "With me it's all or nothing, Ian. Give it all to me." God, he'd wanted to give her all of him. Instead he'd given her nothing and he bitterly regretted it.

No more regrets. Not after tonight.

Ian lifted his hips with small pulses, thrusting gently in and out of her mouth. Everything in his body from the waist down felt so tight it could pop, like a violin string wound too many times around the peg. He leaned back on his elbows to ease the pressure, but Flash was relentless, drawing him into her mouth again and again, sucking hard, licking harder. Every time she moaned he felt the vibrations all through his body from her throat to his.

A hot red flush burned across his chest. The room felt a million degrees and then some. Blood pounded in his ears. His vision swam as he looked up at the ceiling where the north wall met the south wall in a triangle. Dizzy with desire, he looked down the length of his body at Flash and watched her mouth moving up and down his cock with a look of bliss on her face. Mistake. Big mistake.

"Stop," Ian said.

Immediately Flash stopped and sat back. Slowly Ian sat straight up again and breathed a few times to clear his cloudy head. His throat was dry from breathing so hard.

"You almost made me come," he said.

"Oh, no," she said. "How awful."

"It is awful, and I don't think you're nearly as sorry as you should be."

"It was very naughty of me," she said, her eyes briefly meeting his before she lowered her gaze again. "You told me not to make you come, and I kept going even though I knew you were close. But it felt too good, having you in my mouth again. I'm sorry."

"Forgiven." He brushed a stray lock of red hair off her forehead. Her hair was only about four inches long and soft as silk on his fingers. Some days she'd put gel in it and style it like a punk star. Today it was free of product and swept back off her face, making her look far more innocent than a woman who could suck cock like Flash should look. He would never, ever tell anyone Flash had this submissive side to her, that she got off on being used sexually by a dominant man. And she would never tell anybody he got off on it as much as she did. It was between him and her. Their dirty, sexy little secret.

"What should I do with you now?" he asked as he laid his hands on each side of her neck and pressed his thumbs into the hollow of her throat. He didn't do it hard, certainly not hard enough to hurt, but only hard enough so she felt him touch her in her most vulnerable spots. Her head fell back a little, her eyelashes fluttered again. She was never more beautiful to him than when he had her on her knees before him, making her his sexual property, if only for a night.

"Fuck me," she said.

"I had a feeling that's what you'd say. One little problem—you have your clothes on."

"I can solve that problem."

"Solve it, then. I'd love to see your solution."

"Am I allowed to stand up?" she asked.

"You are right now. You'll be on your knees again before the night's over, though."

"I'll consider myself warned."

She stood up and pulled her T-shirt off, dropping it on the floor at his feet. She wore a black lace bra under her white shirt, another thing she did that drove him wild. The bra came off in a second and landed at his feet to join her shirt. Her nipples were hard already, dark with desire. He caught one in his mouth when she put her hands on his shoulders to steady herself while kicking off her shoes. Once he had his mouth on her nipple she froze, letting him suck her as hard as she'd sucked him. He held her by the hips as he ran his tongue in circles around her aureole before catching her nipple between his lips again and drawing it into his mouth. She sighed blissfully and wrapped her arms around his shoulders, pulling him closer to him. He took both her breasts in his hands and squeezed them, lightly at first and then harder. Her back arched into his palms. A warm scent of arousal and baby oil rose off her body, a unique mix that had him burying his face in the valley between her breasts and inhaling deep.

She kissed the top of his head.

He felt it, soft as a butterfly landing and taking off again an instant later, but it could have been a brick for how hard the tenderness of it hit him.

"You aren't like this with anyone else, are you?" she asked so softly someone standing in the corner of the room might not have heard her.

"Only you," he said. "I didn't even know I wanted it like this until you. Until you told me how you liked it."

"You knew. You just didn't want to know."

"It scares me a little," he confessed, a hard thing for a man to say to any woman, especially to the one woman whose good opinion mattered more than anything to him. She brought out an animal side of him he'd never let out of its cage before, and since that night, he hadn't been able to put it back.

"Don't be afraid," she said. "I'll protect you."

Their eyes met and she caressed his left cheek with her knuckles. The expression on her face was one of utter adoration. If he hadn't known better, he might have thought it was love.

He latched on to her nipple again, sucking hard while he roughly pushed her jeans and panties down her thighs. She stepped back, kicked them off her ankles, and he ran his hands hard up and down her back, scoring her smooth skin with his fingernails. Her back arched into his mouth and her fingers clutched at his shirt. Without warning her first, he stopped and stood up. He moved behind her and pushed her forward, bending her over the bed. With his knees he nudged her legs apart and made her stand there, spread out for him, on display.

"Are you wet?" he asked as he laid his hand on her hip and rubbed her naked thigh and perfect ass.

"I can answer that question with a question."

"What question?"

"Are you in the room with me?"

"So that's a yes," Ian said. Still...it didn't hurt to find out for himself, firsthand. He touched the lips of her vagina and found them hot and swollen to the touch. Gently he teased them with light touches before spreading them apart and looking at her hole. He ran one fingertip around her, feeling the wetness, how slick she was, how hot and ready for him.

"Please, Ian," she said. She'd buried her face in her crossed arms on the pillow on his bed but he could hear the desperation in her voice loud and clear.

"Please what?" he asked. "Please this?" He pushed two fingers deep inside her. The sound that came out of her shook the rafters. He wanted to hear it again so he spread his fingers apart inside her, opening her wide. Again she made that sound, the combination of a sigh and a groan. He spread her open again, feeling her inner muscles clenching and contracting as he touched sensitive spots inside her. He pushed in as deep as he could with the tips of his two fingers, making her feel him in the pit of her stomach, making her feel things she'd only ever feel with him so that even if she left him, ran away from him and this—whatever it was—she would remember how he made her feel and she would come back to him to feel it again and again and again because he was the one man who could give it to her.

Flash gave a little cry as he pushed in a third and

fourth finger into her body. He felt the muscles twitch and flinch around his hand.

"Ian…"

"Tell me what you want."

"I need to come so much it hurts."

"You need my cock." Not a question, a statement of fact. She didn't dispute it.

"Yes."

"I like it when you need my cock this much. But if I give it to you, then you won't want it anymore when I'm done."

"I can promise you this—I'll always want it."

He took his cock in his hand and pressed it against her wet cleft but didn't enter her. That would be too easy for her, too quick to give her what she wanted. Instead he simply let her feel it. She pushed her hips back against him and his eyes briefly rolled back in his head at the unexpected rush of electric pleasure that ran from his cock up his spine and down again. He nearly lost control and slammed all eight inches of him into her right then and there.

"You make me want to do very bad things to you," he said.

She laughed softly, seductively. He nearly came from that sound alone.

"Good."

"You're a bad influence on me," he said, rubbing the throbbing tip of his penis against her labia.

"Oh, no. What if your daddy tells us we can't play together anymore?"

"There are worse things in life than being an orphan."

When she tried to laugh, Ian stopped her by sticking his fingers in her again. The laugh turned to a gasp.

She buried her face in her arms again and made soft noises as he stroked her inside. He couldn't get enough of her. When he took his fingers out he licked her wetness off them. She tasted both sweet and bitter and Ian knew, before long, he would bury his tongue inside her to taste every drop.

But first he had to fuck her or they were both going to die from the need.

He left her bent over the bed to retrieve the condoms from the side table drawer.

"You keep handcuffs in there, too?" Flash asked.

"No. Should I?"

"Just trying to figure out what to get you as a Hanukkah gift."

Ian walked to her, laid his hand on her lower back and stroked her from the base of her spine to her neck and down again.

Ian pulled off his T-shirt and yanked down his jeans, kicking them to the corner of the room where he hoped they would remain for all night. Even better, all year.

He rolled on the condom and opened her up again with his fingers. She pushed back against his hand again, signaling how much she wanted him. As if he didn't know already.

"Crawl forward on the bed," he said. "But stay on your stomach."

She did as he instructed, lying prone on his black sheets. He grabbed his thickest pillow and lifted her up by the hips, placing it under her pelvis.

"Comfortable?" he asked.

"Very."

"Good. Stay comfortable. You're going to be there awhile."

He loved that he could say stuff like that to her without scaring her or offending her. He'd been shocked by how easily it came to him when she told him what she liked, more shocked by how much he'd missed it when it was gone.

When he had her in position, her body open to him, her back arched in eagerness, he entered her slowly, an inch at a time. He wasn't trying to tease her so much as he wanted to go slow, relish every second of sliding his cock into her again for the first time since that night, that wild night, that perfect night. He sighed with unabashed pleasure as he filled her. Flash moaned as he went deep, a sound he wanted to burn into his ears so he could hear it every day of his life. He leaned forward and grasped her by the shoulders and started to thrust. She was burning hot all around him and soft, too, so soft and welcoming he felt like his cock was being enveloped by her body, pulled in deeper and held.

"Tell me how it feels," he said.

"So good."

"You can do better than that. I was specific."

"You're thick," she said.

"Rude." He playfully swatted her ass and she yelped in pain.

"Your *cock* is thick," she said.

"I knew what you meant. I just wanted an excuse to slap your ass. Not that I need an excuse."

"Never."

"Go on. This is getting interesting," he said. "My cock is thick and…"

"It stretches me out when it's first inside me." She turned her head to the side so he could see her face and hear her better. "It's something almost like pain but it's not actual pain. It's sharp like pain, intense like pain, but it doesn't hurt. It's the opposite of hurting."

"Fascinating. And…?"

She grinned, and he could tell she was having as much fun with this game as he was. That's how she'd explained it to him when they'd been making out like horny teenagers in the elevator of his building that night on the way up to his apartment.

Play a game with me tonight, Ian. Here are the rules. You tell me anything and everything you want me to do or say and I'll do it and I'll say it.

That's the game? he'd asked. *How do we know who wins?*

She answered with the sexiest smile he'd ever seen— *That's the best part about the game. If we both play, we both win…*

"My pussy wants to push it out when you start pushing it in. I can feel the muscles tightening so I have to breathe to keep from bearing down and squeezing. But once you're all the way in me, it's like my muscles are trying to keep you in."

"I can feel it," he said, thrusting slowly as they spoke. Just hearing her talk about his cock inside her was bringing him right to the edge of orgasm. But he squeezed her sculpted shoulders, breathed shallow breaths and focused on her.

"Does it feel good?" she asked.

"Your pussy holding my cock inside you? Yeah, you could say it feels kind of good."

She grinned again. He was falling in love with that grin. Making her smile that big was nearly as sexy as hearing her talk about his cock.

"I'm glad it feels good on your cock. I want my

body to make you happy. Yours makes me happy. And relieved."

"Relieved?"

"You pushing your cock in me for the first time in six months? I'd say 'profound fucking relief' is one way to explain it. You know that feeling when you've been standing for almost eight straight hours and your legs are aching and your back is tired and your feet hurt and then you sink into the most comfortable soft leather chair in the world and you groan it feels so good to finally get to sit down?"

"I know that feeling."

"It's just like that but inside my vagina."

Ian laughed. Flash was tough and she wasn't easy to impress, but damn, she knew how to pay a guy a compliment.

"You miss this." He punctuated the sentence with a long deep thrust.

"Every day," she sighed. "Every day and every night."

Ian leaned forward and kissed her between her shoulder blades. He loved fucking her while she lay on her stomach not only because of how dominant he felt in the position but because how beautiful her back was. She had a full-back tattoo, ink from her shoulders to her hips in the form of the night sky with the moon, stars and the Orion constellation. It was a work of art, lovely in its simplicity, strange in its reversal of colors. On Flash's back, the sky was her pale skin and the stars were black ink, not the other way around.

"Ian..." she sighed as he kissed the back of her neck. He loved her short hair, loved how it gave him such easy access to her neck and earlobes. Her scent was addictive, her taste intoxicating. He was so aroused he ached from his thighs to his stomach. The tension was unbearable but he bore it because he wasn't ready to let go of it yet. He was rock hard inside her and he could come any second. But still he held back, waiting, wanting to stay inside of her as long as he could. He rode her hard, his hands on her back to steady himself while he thrust into her. She was soaking wet. He could hear it, feel it... She was soaking his pillow. He'd sleep on that pillow tonight just to breathe the scent of her.

"How do you want it?" he asked her.

"You know how," she said softly. He did and he was more than happy to oblige. When his hips were at the tightest, his cock so hard it hurt, he pulled out of her and rolled the condom off and tossed it. With his left hand holding her left hip, he stroked himself with his right hand. He pumped his hips into his own fingers, pushing and pushing, the tension building to the breaking point. And then finally...at last...he let it break.

With a gasp, he came, semen spurting onto her back as waves of pleasure rolled through him, knocking the breath out of him. After the last spasm of release shot through him, he sat forward on his hands and knees, his head hanging between his arms as he caught his breath. When his vision cleared, he looked down and saw her beautiful back that he had marked.

"I added to your decor," he said between breaths.

"Does my night sky look like the Milky Way now?"

"You're so gross," he said, laughing.

"You know you love it."

"I do. Flip over."

"I'll get it all over your sheets."

"Do as you're told," he said, slapping her ass again.

She obeyed at once, turning onto her back and lying flat underneath him. He dropped his head to suck her nipples again. She arched her breasts into his mouth and he sucked steadily as he sought her clitoris with his fingertips. It was easy to find, not only because she was so swollen but because she had a piercing there. He gently tugged the metal bar of her piercing and Flash flinched with pleasure, gasping his name. He rubbed the swollen knot of flesh in slow circles while licking her breasts. That knot throbbed and pulsed and he couldn't stop himself from lowering his head between her thighs and lapping at it with his tongue. It only took seconds to get her there. Her hips rose off the bed and she came with a loud cry. Ian kissed his way up her body, lingering over her hips and stomach and breasts.

"Are you done for?" he asked.

She nodded.

"Take a breather. You've earned it. I'll keep playing."

She nodded again, the slightest smile on her lips. She loved letting him use her body. She'd told him that six months ago and the words *Use my body and my holes any way you want, Ian* still rang in his ears.

He carefully straddled her stomach and sat on her hips. He took her breasts in his hands and massaged them, squeezed them, palmed them and lifted them while she lay there with her eyes closed, recovering.

"You enjoyed that," he said.

"You know I did."

"What should I do to you now? So many options. I could fuck you again, eat you out, make you go down on me... I'm open to suggestions."

"You did promise me dinner and a beer yesterday,"

she said. "I didn't get my pub food or my beer and you just fucked me right through the dinner hour."

"Typical. Just typical," he said with a sigh as he climbed off her and grabbed his jeans off the floor. As soon as she'd mentioned dinner, his stomach reminded him he hadn't eaten in hours. "All you women think about is sex and food and beer. What about my needs, Flash?"

"What are your needs?"

"Beer and food," he said. "So get your ass in gear."

"Yes, boss." She climbed out of bed, wincing and smiling in that order. "You're buying, right?"

"I can answer that question with a question." He paused to kiss her on the mouth because there was nothing sexier than kissing a beautiful naked woman who'd just crawled out of his bed.

"What's the question?"

"Are you spreading for me again later?" he asked. She smiled.

"Dinner's on you," she said.

6

FLASH TOOK A last swallow of her stout and put the beer glass down on the table with a definitive thunk.

"I'm done," she said.

"After two?" Ian shook his head in playful disgust.

"You want me to spread for you later, two is my limit. I need to be awake for that."

He shrugged. "You don't *need* to be awake for it. Technically."

Flash laughed so hard she snorted, which made her laugh even harder. The way Ian had said "technically" had hit her funny bone. She would blame the beer. Yeah, probably the beer. He handed her a napkin since she was clearly in danger of something weird coming out of her nose and she muttered a nasal "Thank you" as she pulled herself together.

"That was a horrible thing to say, wasn't it?" he said, grinning and clearly proud of himself for making her snort-laugh. "Please don't tell HR I said that."

"Never."

"I had a girlfriend once tell me during sex, 'If I fall

asleep you can keep going. I don't mind.' We broke up shortly after that. You okay?"

"Fine. Sorry," she said, putting the beer glass far away from her reach. "Had a little dork moment there."

"Don't be sorry," Ian said, smiling. "It's good to see you being a dork. I didn't know you had it in you."

"Of course I have it in me."

"You're so much cooler than I am, it's depressing," he said.

She rolled her eyes and sat back in their booth at the pub. They'd both eaten so much greasy pub food there was a very good chance that the next round of sex would need to be delayed an hour or two. *Sex was like swimming*, Ian had said. *You have to wait at least twenty minutes after eating before you get back in the pool—or the pussy—as the case may be.*

"How am I cool?" she demanded. "And in what way am I cooler than you? You have money, a ski chalet, and you're, you know, acceptable looking."

"Acceptable? Thank you. My cock has never been harder in its life."

"You're welcome. Now answer the question."

Ian looked at her over the top of his pint glass. He was an IPA man, which she could respect, although she found IPAs too hoppy for her taste.

"You have tattoos of sexy women on your biceps like a fucking sailor. And you have the punk hair. And you drive the little punk truck. And you're a welder. Not just an artist welder, but like an actual welder. That's cool."

"I think you're confusing 'cool' with 'poor.' The truck was the only truck I could afford. I weld for a living—or did—because it was the only job I could find that paid better than minimum wage. I have short hair because it's less likely to get caught in my helmet. As for the tattoos…well, okay, those are cool. You got me there."

"They are. I used to want to get tattooed but Dad would have killed me. By the time I was old enough to do it without Dad flipping his shit, I'd grown out of the desire to have one."

"Your body is perfect. It doesn't need ink."

"Your body is perfect. Why did you get ink?"

"I wanted it." She shrugged. "No other reason. Love Bettie Page. Love Rosie the Riveter. They're my wing-women. Rosie reminds me to work hard. Bettie reminds me to play hard. They were badass before women were allowed to be badass. And that's badass."

"Cute team—Bettie and Veronica."

"That's who I was named after."

"Are you serious? You're named for the girl in the Archie comics?"

She rolled her eyes and nodded. "Better Veronica than Betty, right? No offense," she said to her Bettie Page bicep tattoo. "I'm talking about a different Betty. Who were you named after?"

"Ian Fleming."

"The guy who wrote the James Bond books?"

"He's Dad's favorite author. It could have been worse. He almost did name me James Bond Asher. That would have been a lot to live up to."

"Your dad doesn't strike me as a James Bond kind of guy."

"He's not," Ian said. "He's the opposite of James Bond. No risks. No danger. No seducing beautiful women. He never even remarried after my mother died. He's dated some, but not much. He's more interested in my personal life than having one of his own. I let him set me up on three blind dates over the past six months. That was probably a mistake but I had a certain red-haired welder I was trying to get over. Didn't work. One date each. No second date. Dad was more disappointed it didn't work out than I was."

"Who were these women?"

"Just women he knew. Daughters of friends."

"Fancy daughters of rich friends?"

Ian shrugged.

"Ian?"

"Yeah, kind of," he said. "One was a professor, one was a doctor, one was a lawyer."

"Quite a triumvirate you had there."

"They were nice," Ian said noncommittally. "They were pretty, too, and fun. I couldn't stop thinking about you the entire time I was with them. No second dates."

"A professor, a doctor and a lawyer. And I didn't even go to college."

"I don't care," Ian said.

"Where did you go to college?" she asked.

"Flash, it doesn't matter. I don't care about where you or I went to school."

"I know where you went to college," Flash said. "Starts with an *H* and ends with an *arvard*."

"So?"

"Your father is very proud of his Harvard-educated son."

"He is."

"He's not going to like us going out, is he?"

"He won't care. Now that you're not an employee anymore, I mean."

"You sure about that?"

"I'm thirty-six, Flash."

"You're also his only child and you're going to inherit the whole Asher empire, right? You don't think your father is going to have a problem with you and me?"

"Dad wants the best for me. If dating you is the best for me, then he's going to be happy."

"We're dating now?"

"I'd like you to be my girlfriend. I wanted it six months ago. I want it now. You don't have to tell me an answer now. I'm only asking you to think about it."

"I'll think about it."

She squeezed his hand and smiled. It felt good to do this, to hold hands across a table in public where anyone could see them. Not that anyone was paying them any attention. At work Ian was money, suits, clean-cut—the boss-man—while she lived in her dirty work clothes, her welding helmet and made eighteen bucks an hour. Worlds apart…but not here, not now. He wore jeans and a T-shirt. She wore jeans and a T-shirt. His hair was all sexy and disheveled from his gray knit winter hat and hers was equally disheveled from being bounced around his bed. They looked like the sort of people who'd hang out in a pub on Mount Hood. They looked like a couple. She liked it. She liked him. She'd been in love with him for a long time. Nice to finally like him a little bit, too.

The waitress came by and cleared off their plates and refilled their water glasses. Ian ordered the Oregon blackberry cobbler for two, and told the waitress "thank you" and "no rush." Flash had waitressed to pay for her art classes when she was eighteen and nineteen and ever since she'd judged people based on their behavior toward waitstaff. Ian passed that test.

"You ordered dessert?" she asked. "After all that food?"

"Haven't eaten since breakfast. You're going to help me, right?"

"I'll try but no promises. Why did I eat all those fries?"

"Because they serve Portland ketchup here."

She pointed at him. "That's right. It was either eat the fries or drink that stuff straight from the bottle."

"I knew you'd like this place. It's the sole reason why I moved up here. The snow and forest and skiing and all that boring shit had nothing to do with it. Just the food."

"You're a wise man, Ian Asher."

His eyes widened.

"What?" she asked.

"Sorry. Still can't get used to you being nice to me. It's jarring."

She winced and sighed. "Yeah, I was pretty rough on you. You deserved it but still…maybe I overdid it a little."

"It's fine," he said. He picked up his napkin and started shredding it. A nervous habit? She liked that she could make him a little nervous even after the snort-laughing incident. "But I have to ask…you're really quitting because you want the new job, right? You aren't quitting because of what happened between us?"

"I'm quitting because I want the new job," Flash said. "Here's the thing…that menorah I made for you—it's the first time I've sculpted anything in months. I've been tired from work, distracted, depressed, discouraged, angry… I didn't have the emotional or physical energy to do any sculpting. It's a horrible feeling to be cut off from the one thing that makes me feel like a real human being."

"I'm sorry you've been in such a bad place."

"It's not your fault."

"It isn't?"

"Well…not entirely your fault. I'd be lying if I said the breakup wasn't part of why I've been in a bad place. But there's a lot more to it. I've had an installation up at the Morrison Gallery in Portland for six months and I haven't sold a single piece. Not one. It's not like I do the sculpting for the money. That's not the point. The point is that when someone buys your art, it's validation. You draw a picture for your parents and they put it on the fridge because that's what parents do. Doesn't matter if it's the drawing of your house and your trees looks like cat barf, Little Junior drew it so it goes on the fridge. But when a stranger, a total stranger, plunks down ten thousand dollars on a sculpture you made, it's better than anything. It's better than sex."

"Better than sex?"

She nodded. "A lot of people on this planet get laid. Not that many people on this planet can sell their works of art for ten thousand dollars or more."

"That's true. I just got laid and I can't sculpt to save my life."

"It's my life's work, being a sculptor," she said. "Having your entire life's work validated…it's the single most important thing to me. Art is my religion."

"I'm not an artist but I kind of understand wanting that. One of Dad's good friends owns a huge construction company in Seattle. He tried to hire me out from under Dad. Offered me a big raise, big office, all that. I had to turn it down, otherwise Dad would have a heart attack, but it was one of those great moments when you realize you're genuinely good at what you do. This guy wasn't my father. I'm not his son. And he still looked at my work and said, 'Yes, this is the guy we want and I'm willing to risk a thirty-year-old friendship to have Ian Asher come work for me because Ian Asher is that good.' It was validating."

"You get it."

"I get it," he said. "So… I guess you won't let me buy one of your sculptures from the gallery?"

"If you did, I would never see you again," she said, meaning every single word of it.

"What if instead of buying one of your sculptures, I broke in and stole one?"

She thought about that, rubbed her chin, narrowed her eyes and finally nodded.

"Not a bad idea. It would get my name in the papers. Art theft is a huge international crime. But I have a better idea. You tell me what to make and I'll try to make it."

"You don't have to—"

"I want to. Making your menorah was the first time I'd felt real joy in months. Something about creating it for you, specifically for you, really got my juices flowing."

He raised his eyebrow.

"My *other* juices," she clarified. "I think you're my muse. So a-muse me, muse. Give me an idea and I'll give it a shot. Challenge me."

Ian went silent for a moment. She'd put him on the spot but she didn't feel bad about it. Inspiration often came in sudden flashes, sudden epiphanies. Of course those sudden epiphanies often resulted in weeks and months of grueling work turning those bolts from the blue into art, but it was worth it to her. The art was worth it.

He reached into his back pocket and pulled out his wallet. They hadn't brought the bill yet so she couldn't imagine why he'd need his wallet. He dug through a stack of cards and small papers until he produced a photograph. He held it out to her and she took it from his hand.

The picture was of a woman smiling at the camera. It looked posed, like a yearbook photograph. She was a beautiful young lady with wavy hair with Ian's mouth and eyes. While the picture was posed her smile was bright and natural. She was a happy woman.

"This is Ivy? This is your mother?" she asked.

Ian nodded. "It's the only picture I have of her. It was from her and Dad's college yearbook."

"You cut it out of the yearbook?"

"No, Dad would have killed me. I waited until he was out of town one weekend, and I took the yearbook to a copy center and had them make a copy of it on photo paper. Pathetic, right? I was eighteen and too much of a coward to ask my father to give me a photograph of my own mother."

"That's not cowardly," she said. "It's very sweet. It must be hard for you not knowing her."

"It's hard. I keep trying to work up the guts to ask Dad to help me contact my mother's parents but I haven't yet. It's a real tender spot for him."

"I can imagine," she said. She knew all about parental sore spots.

"Anyway... I love the menorah. It's perfect. But you can't keep that up all year. What I'd love to have is something around to remind me of her." He pointed at the photograph. "Something to honor her, I guess? Something to keep her present? She's nothing but an outline in my mind. It would be nice to have something more than the bare bones, more than an outline. That's probably too much to ask. You don't know any more about her than I do."

Flash studied the picture a little longer. This was a big challenge—creating a metal sculpture to honor Ian's mother. She didn't sculpt the human form. Nature was her subject—she made aluminum roses and orchids, copper sunflowers, cherry trees in bloom made of pure steel. But a woman? She'd never sculpted a woman before. Could she? Should she? She didn't even know this woman. Or did she? This woman, hardly more than a kid, had eloped with her lover over the extreme disapproval of both their families, and she'd done it at the age of eighteen and had a baby all without any family support. The very thought of trying something like that terrified Flash. Whoever Ivy was she had a backbone of steel to do something like that.

A backbone of steel?

Yes. That. A backbone of steel.

Her brain lit up and her fingers tingled…images floated through her mind—lines, turns, light glancing off metal, curves…beautiful metal curves… She felt a rush of adrenaline. She wanted to dash home right now and get to work, but she knew better than that. The idea had to percolate a little more, coalesce, take form, bring itself to life and introduce itself. And as soon as it did, then she'd get to work.

Flash returned the photograph to Ian.

"I have an idea," she said, looking up at Ian and smiling. "But I'll need your help with it."

Ian winced and looked immediately uncomfortable.

"I...I'm not really very good at the welding stuff. I've done it a little and—"

"Don't worry. I don't need your help making it. I can do that."

"Then what do you need me to do?"

"I'll need you to take some pictures of me—naked."

Ian nodded. The waitress came to their table bearing their dessert. Ian smiled up at her.

"If you don't mind, we're going to need that to go."

"YOU'RE ENJOYING THIS too much," Flash said as Ian placed his hand on her left hip and shifted it to the right. He moved her chin two inches to the left and then back one inch again to the right. She and Ian were in his living room and he had her standing by the bare patch of wall by the large stone fireplace while he took pictures of her with her own cell phone to use in the creation of her next sculpture. After twenty pictures she'd declared they had more than enough to work with but Ian wasn't quite finished posing her.

"You're naked. I'm taking pictures of you. Can you please explain how the hell I'm supposed to enjoy it less?"

"This isn't supposed to be sexual. It's for art."

"Of course it is. Art is what I named my cock."

Flash reached behind her and cupped Ian between the legs.

"Hi, Art."

"Art says hello," Ian said. "He's looking forward to spending more time with you."

"What a nice guy. Let me see the last pics," she said.

Ian returned her phone to her and she flipped through the pictures while he peered over her shoulder.

"I like that one," he said, pointing at one particular picture where Flash had her back to the camera and bore all her weight on one foot while she looked to the side.

"Venus de Milo pose," she said. "Very classic."

"Classics are classics for a reason."

"We're going to delete that one right there," she said, pulling up one picture Ian had taken of nothing but her ass.

"Oh, no, that's my favorite."

"Fine, fine." She texted him the picture and then deleted it. "Happy now?"

"Art and I are grateful. We done?" He sounded a little sad about that.

"I have plenty to work with here."

"So do I." Ian wrapped his arms around her from behind and cupped her breasts in his large hands.

"You're fondling me again," she said.

"I'm fond of fondling."

"Did you want to do this at work?"

"Fondling you was the least of what I wanted to do to you every single day at work. But I behaved myself. It was horrible."

"Behaving sucks," she said.

"I suck," he said, and started sucking on her earlobe. It tickled so much she laughed and Ian had to subdue her giggles with a sharp bite. "I like you hanging around my house completely naked. I might institute a dress code here."

"An *un*dressed code?"

"Excellent idea," he said.

"You're violating your own dress code, Mr. Asher. You have all your clothes on."

"I'm barefoot."

"Doesn't count."

"I'm the boss around here, remember? I decide what counts and what doesn't count," he said into her ear.

She closed her eyes and shivered in his arms. She loved when he talked like that to her, loved when he got tough with her, ordered her around, acted like the boss of her. He was so good at it, such a natural. His right hand slid from her breast down her stomach and cupped her between the legs. He lightly stroked her as he dropped soft kisses along her naked shoulder. It felt so good it was dizzying and she had to reach out and put her hand flat against the wall to hold herself steady. His left hand tugged at her nipples, lightly pinched and rolled them between his fingers, while his right hand rubbed her clitoris. He rocked his hips into her, making their bodies move together as he teased and fondled and caressed her most tender spots. He slid a finger inside her and she flinched with pleasure, moaned with it, dripped with it.

"You're going to come for me, aren't you?" he asked into her ear again.

"Yes," she said, hissing the word between clenched teeth. Her lower back was so tight with delicious tension it ached.

"Spread your legs a little more. More...perfect," he said as she shifted her feet apart until her stance met with his approval.

He pulled his wet finger out of her and used it to rub her clitoris again. She was already swollen, already aching, already ready. Her breasts felt full and heavy from his attention and her skin wore a hot flush of red. Ian's lips caressed the back of her neck and she relished the feel of his hot breath on her flesh.

"You have any idea how hard you make me?" he asked into her ear. "You have any idea how hard it was to see you every day at work and know I couldn't have you?"

"Probably as hard for you as it was for me."

"So you had to jack off in the shower when you got home from work, too?"

"You think guys are the only people who masturbate?"

"You got off thinking about me?"

"Ian... I call my vibrator 'The Boss.'"

"Don't take this the wrong way, Flash, but...I'm so fucking happy you quit your job."

When she started to laugh he pushed two fingers into her again and her laugh died in her throat and was reborn a moan.

With both Ian's hands between her legs, penetrating her and stroking her at the same time, it was a miracle she could still stand. She put both hands on the wall to hold herself upright as he worked her clitoris and fucked her with his fingers. Her body felt so open, so wet and tender and alive. He made her feel alive like no man she'd been with before. Past lovers had played at being boss, but Ian really was the boss. He had real power in this world, real authority, and something in her responded to that like she was born to be his. Her upbringing had been chaotic, always running, always moving. But Ian was so steady, so strong, so manly and solid, she wanted to put herself entirely in his hands— her body, her trust, her heart. But especially her body.

Ian slipped a third finger inside of her and her pussy

contracted around his probing hand. He chuckled and she wanted to step on his foot for laughing at her.

"I love playing with your body," he said. "You're my favorite toy. And my favorite toy needs to come. Doesn't she?"

"She does…" Flash breathed.

"Come for me, then," he said, still rubbing and stroking her. The fingers inside her moved in a circle, hitting every nerve ending, sending spikes of pleasure shooting through her stomach to her hard tight nipples.

"Anything you say, boss."

She pushed her hips forward and against his hand. She pushed again and Ian curled his fingers inside her to make her moan again. He fucked her faster now with his fingers, rubbed her harder while her hips pumped with a desperate rhythm. Ian whispered dirty words of encouragement while he pushed her closer to that delicious edge. Her stomach knotted up and her fingers on the wall curled into fists. When she couldn't take it anymore, it finally happened. She cried out as her pleasure peaked. She felt a shattering inside her as the tension released all at once. Her inner muscles fluttered wildly around Ian's fingers, muscles pulsed against his touch. It was pure ecstasy and all Ian's doing.

When her orgasm finally faded, Flash hung limp and spent in Ian's arms while he kissed and bit her neck and shoulders.

"Stay," he ordered, and she had neither the will nor the energy to disobey. She pressed her palms against the wall again to stay vertical as Ian undressed behind her and put on a condom. With one thrust he entered her from behind, splitting her open and driving into the core of her. He pumped his cock into her hard and fast, harder and faster than he ever had before. It was rough and wild, hungry and desperate. She loved it. She loved it as much as she loved him, and the only thing she hated was that she was too scared to tell him that. He made her feel too much. Her love was equal to her fear so she stayed silent as he fucked her, silent as he fondled her, silent as he came in her.

They stood by the wall, their bodies still joined as Ian rested his forehead on her shoulder.

"Did that hurt?" he asked.

"Only in the good way."

"I'm never like this with anyone but you," he said as he caught his breath. She loved hearing him out of breath from fucking her. "You bring out the worst in me. Or the best. Can't tell sometimes."

"I bring out the you in you."

"You like me like this, don't you?"

She loved him like this. But she couldn't say that. Not yet anyway.

"More than you know, Ian."

"Try that again."

Flash laughed tiredly.

"More than you know...boss."

7

FLASH FINALLY MADE it home around midnight. Ian had tried to talk her into staying, but she wasn't quite ready for that yet. Better to leave him wanting more than wear out her welcome. She parked in her usual space across from Mrs. Scheinberg's front door and saw the living room light shining through the curtains. Curious, Flash knocked softly on the front door.

Only a few seconds later Mrs. Scheinberg opened the door.

"Yes, dear?" Mrs. Scheinberg asked. She wore her favorite blue silk pajamas, the ones with the mandarin collar, and her matching blue bathrobe.

"I just saw your light was on. What are you doing still up?"

"Couldn't sleep."

"Something wrong?"

"I'm an old woman. That's what's wrong. You want to come in?"

Flash followed her inside and locked up behind them.

"You're home late," Mrs. Scheinberg said as she went into the kitchen and put her teakettle on the stove.

"I was with Ian."

"With him or *with* him?"

"Both."

"Oh, my…" Mrs. Scheinberg turned around and gave her a smile. "I take it your gift went over well."

"That might be an understatement."

"So why are you here? Shouldn't you be there?" She nodded her head toward the kitchen window that faced east to Mount Hood.

Flash shrugged as she took her usual seat at Mrs. Scheinberg's pale blue Formica kitchen table.

"He asked me to stay the night. He wanted me to. I thought it would be better if I didn't push my luck."

"Playing hard to get. The oldest trick in the book." Mrs. Scheinberg nodded her approval. "I've done it myself. Works every time."

"I don't know if that's it. I just don't want to get too serious too fast."

"You're in love with him and have been for months. How much more serious can you get?"

Flash sat back in the chair, stretching out her legs under the table. Her hips were tight from the sex, not that she'd complain. The best kind of pain, in her opinion.

"He doesn't know I'm in love with him. He doesn't need to know that."

"Why won't you tell him?" Mrs. Scheinberg asked as she dug her Christmas cookies out of what looked to Flash like a box that had once stored Brillo pads. Clever lady. "You're worried he doesn't love you?"

"He doesn't act like he's in love with me. Lust, yes. But I can't get over the feeling that the sex is the only reason he wants me around. He said something tonight about me being the only woman he's 'himself' with."

"That's a compliment."

"He said it while we were having sex. He wasn't talking about sharing his heart or his soul or his hobbies. He meant I'm the only girl he can have the kind of sex with he likes to have. I think he's only dated nice girls before."

"Look at me, darling." Mrs. Scheinberg patted the table in front of Flash and then pointed at her own face. "I'm going to tell you a true thing, as true as two and two is four. I'm not your grandmother. I'm not your mother. I'm sixty-two years older than you are. And still, every day you come and see me and not just a knock on the door to make sure I'm still alive. You bring me my cookies, you spend time with me. My last dear friend died two years ago and it was a lonely time for me. Very lonely. And then you came along, and I'm not so lonely anymore. Veronica Redding, if you're not a nice girl I don't know what one is."

Flash smiled and swallowed a lump in her throat.

"Thank you," she said, smiling. "But you know what I'm saying."

Mrs. Scheinberg clucked her tongue and pushed a plate of cookies across the table to Flash.

"No, I don't. So he's a little wilder with you than he is with other women. What's the harm in that if you both enjoy it, both want it? It just means you're compatible in bed. It hardly means he's using you for sex."

"I want him to use me for sex. I also want him to love me. I'm worried I'm asking for too much."

"It's not too much. He should love you. Why wouldn't he?"

"Ian's family has so much money. His father is a state senator and on top of that he's rich, he's a philanthropist. He's got friends in high places. They're the sort of people who 'hobnob.' I don't even know what hobnobbing is but I know only really rich people do it. The Asher's 'winter' in the Mediterranean. I've never dated anybody before who uses 'winter' as a verb."

"It's winter now, and your Ian is still here."

"First of all, it's not winter until December 21. Second, he doesn't go to the Mediterranean in winter. But his dad does and Ian will someday. He's Dean Asher's only son and Dean Asher runs an empire."

Mrs. Scheinberg waved her hand dismissively.

"Nonsense. The Roman Empire was an empire. The Ottoman Empire was an empire. The Asher empire is an outlet mall. Dean Asher owns some very successful businesses. He doesn't rule the world. You shouldn't be intimidated by him."

"I know. That's Ian's world though, and I can't picture myself in it. I can't get over the feeling that Ian's out of my league."

"He's a man. You're a woman. No man is out of any woman's league," Mrs. Scheinberg said. "And don't you forget it. And if Ian Asher doesn't believe that, too, you bring him over here and I'll tell him."

"You just want to meet him in person."

"Can you blame me? I love a man with blue eyes."

"He does have pretty eyes," Flash said, nodding. "Pretty everything." She buried her face in her hands and groaned. "I hate being in love with someone who's not in love with me." She laughed at herself and dropped her hands to her lap.

"Don't believe what people say about men being

only interested in sex. Men want love as much as women do. I had a father, three brothers, one husband and two sons and every last one of them loved their wives like their lives depended on it. You should give this man a little more credit. It's very possible he's falling in love with you. Don't be surprised if he does. And in the meantime you should be honest with him about your feelings instead of hiding them out of fear."

"I'm scared to not be scared."

Mrs. Scheinberg put her hand over hers and patted it gently.

"I know. He's hurt you before. It's understandable you'd want to protect your heart. It is. But two wrongs don't make a right. Don't play with his heart while you're protecting yours."

"I don't want to play with his heart," Flash said.

"Good girl."

"Just his body."

"Go to bed this instant, young lady." Mrs. Scheinberg pointed at the front door and Flash laughed as she stood up to leave. She reached for the last cookie on the plate, but Mrs. Scheinberg snatched it away from her.

"No more cookies," Mrs. Scheinberg said. "You've been too naughty."

"You remember I buy you those cookies, right?"

Mrs. Scheinberg peered at her through narrowed eyes.

She pushed the plate back slowly toward Flash.

"One more cookie."

"That's more like it," Flash said.

She kissed Mrs. Scheinberg good-night on the cheek and walked upstairs to her apartment. It wasn't much to look at. The "living room" was a workroom where she kept all her metalsmithing supplies stored and sorted. The bathroom was one sink and one shower stall and that was it, and her bedroom had nothing but a bed, an old blue dresser and a closet. Ian had done more with his new place in one month than she'd done with her apartment in two years. All her extra money went into her art supplies. If only she knitted or painted or wrote poetry she might have money to buy some decent furniture. But no, she had to be a metal sculptor and you can't buy scrap metal at Target or Hobby Lobby. Too bad.

She'd just have to keep her fingers crossed one of her pieces would sell soon. If she sold any one of the pieces at the Morrison she could afford a year's worth of supplies. But she wouldn't think about that tonight, not with so many pleasanter things to think about like her evening with Ian.

Flash went to her bathroom, washed her face, brushed her teeth, took out her contacts and was ready to fall asleep the second her head hit the pillow. But she didn't hit the pillow because her gray tabby cat Bob Ross was sound asleep on her pillow already.

"Pathetic," she said, shaking her head at him. He didn't even wake up when she turned the bedroom light on. "Do some housework. Earn your keep."

Bob Ross opened one eye for one second before closing it again.

"Yeah, I figured that was your answer."

She set her phone on her bedside charger and pulled the covers back on her bed. As soon as her head hit the sheets underneath the currently occupied pillow, her phone beeped.

Ian had sent her a text message. She grinned as she read it.

Did you make it home safe? Ian wrote.

Flash texted back quickly. Yes, I'm already in bed.

Did I wake you?

Not asleep yet.

I had fun tonight. More fun than I've had in six months.

Me, too.

Can we have fun tomorrow night?

That can be arranged.

What are you wearing? Ian asked. She'd seen that coming a mile away.

Cat hair.

Hot.

Want me to send you a picture of my pussy?

Yes, please and thank you.

So polite. She loved a man with manners.

"Smile, Bob," Flash said, and took a quick pic of Bob Ross still curled on her pillow looking not unlike a furry doughnut.

She sent the picture to Ian.

Nice, he replied. Daddy likes.

Flash laughed so hard she woke up Bob Ross and he stalked off the bed in a huff.

Do I get a dick pic now? she wrote him.

She waited and a few seconds passed. Finally her phone beeped again.

Dick pic, Ian captioned the photo.

It was a photo of the wildly unsexy face of Richard "Tricky Dick" Nixon.

I am so wet right now, she wrote back.

Good. Mission accomplished. Sleep well.

You, too, she replied, and then thought of one more thing she needed to tell him.

She took a deep breath, summoned her courage and wrote back the answer to a question he'd asked her four hours ago at dinner.

Yes.

Yes, what? Ian wrote back.

Yes, I want to be your girlfriend.

Another long pause followed. Flash caught herself holding her breath.

When the reply came it was nothing but smiley face emojis.

Ian, you're thirty-six years old. Act like it.

He replied with a single frowning face. She laughed so hard she almost cried.

She started writing to tell him that she was sorry and he was allowed to use emojis if he wanted to, but the phone rang before she could finish typing out her message.

"Hey, girlfriend," Ian said as soon as she answered.

"I'm regretting this already."

"Are not."

"Why are you calling me? It's one in the morning?"

"Do I need a reason to call my girlfriend?"

"Yes, at one in the morning you do."

"I have a reason."

"What?"

He laughed on the other end of the line and it was the sort of laugh to make a girl's toes curl up in the Doctor Who knee socks she wore to bed.

"So…what *are* you wearing?"

Flash answered absolutely truthfully this time.

"A smile."

8

IAN DRAGGED HIMSELF out of bed at ten the next morning. Usually he never slept that late. He couldn't. But usually he didn't remodel an entire bathroom in one day and then fuck his new girlfriend three times in one evening and then stay up until two in the morning to have phone sex with her. A man needed his eight hours of sleep after such an eventful day. He rose from bed and pulled on yesterday's jeans and a white T-shirt with the words Asher Construction in strong black letters across the back.

He was halfway down the stairs to the kitchen when he heard the sounds of movement downstairs.

"You back for more already?" Ian called down the steps as he stretched and yawned.

"More what?" his father, Dean Asher, called back. "Or do I not want to know? Although I think I know."

Ian paused on the stairs, winced and rubbed his forehead.

"Ian?"

"Hi, Dad. I forgot you were coming by this morning," Ian said as he squared his shoulders and made his way down to the living room.

"Apparently so. You up for skiing today?"

"I will be. Give me a minute."

"Take all the time you need."

His father was a young-looking fifty-six with pale blond hair very gradually turning gray. Ian remembered last year at the opening day of the local baseball team Asher Construction sponsored that his dad had worn a team T-shirt and a ball cap. One of the coaches had assumed Ian and his father were actually brothers instead of father and son. Ian could only pray he aged as well as his father. But for all the good genes, Dad was still very much Dad and Dad did not look happy with his son this morning.

"Coffee?" His fathered handed him a steaming cup. "Hope you don't mind I made a pot."

"Don't mind," Ian said. "Thank you. I needed this."

"I believe it. You had a late night?" Dean Asher raised his eyebrow.

"Sort of."

"More than sort of, I think. You should clean up after yourself a little better." His father nodded toward the corner of the living room where a condom wrapper lay on the bare floor where he'd fucked Flash after their little photo session. He'd thrown away the condom but must have been too preoccupied with her beautiful naked body to pick up the foil wrapper after they'd finished.

"Oops," Ian said. "You got me. Your son has sex sometimes."

"Where did I go wrong? Anyone I know?" His father took a big sip of his own coffee.

Ian walked over to the sink and turned the water on. He splashed his face with cool water and then cupped his hands to wet his hair with it.

"Veronica Redding," Ian said as he grabbed a dishtowel off the rack to dry his face. He dropped the dishtowel onto the counter, leaned back and waited for his father to pronounce judgment.

"Veronica Redding? You mean Flash Redding? Our welder?"

"That's her. You sound surprised."

"I am. For a couple reasons."

"And those are?"

"Well…quite frankly, I didn't think she liked men." Ian rolled his eyes.

"Sorry," his father said. "Female welder, short hair, got a tattoo of a half-naked lady on her bicep…you assume things."

"Trust me, she likes men. But as Flash would say, you're half-right."

"My apologies for assuming," he said. "However, there is still the little issue of her being an employee of Asher Construction. Unless you've put in your two weeks' notice without telling me about it…"

"Not me, her. She quit two days ago."

"Did she quit because she wanted to quit? Or did she quit because you asked her to quit so you two could…"

"I had no idea she was quitting until she quit. She got a new job and she starts in January. We're pretty much closed down for the month except for the billing department and the interior painting on the office complex in Hood River. She'll get her last paycheck next Friday. For all intents and purposes she is an ex-employee of Asher Construction."

"Well, that's too bad. I hate to lose a good welder. They're not so easy to find."

"Don't think of it as the company losing a welder. Think of it as your son gaining a girlfriend."

"Girlfriend? That sounds pretty serious for two people who have been only dating two days and it better only have been two days." His father was merciless when it came to employees violating company rules. Even when that employee was his own son.

"It's only been two days. Sort of," Ian said.

"Sort of? What do we mean by sort of?"

With a weary sigh, Ian sat down on the leather stool next to the kitchen bar. His father remained standing despite the presence of three other perfectly good stools to sit on. It was much too early to be having this conversation. When his father used the royal "we" nothing good was about to happen.

"What 'we' mean is that Flash and I have had feelings for each other for a long time. We acted on it— one night only—about six months ago. I 'fessed up to Mac Brand, who told me to break it off with her or he'd get rid of both of us, and I did. It didn't happen again. Not until after she quit. That's what I mean by 'sort of.' Satisfied?"

Ian gave all his attention to his coffee while his father turned his back and stared out the window onto the deck and the snow and the mountain.

"Flash Redding is a very good welder," his father said. "I was very happy to have her as an employee of Asher Construction. I would have liked to have had more women on the crew."

"I wouldn't want to do it if I were a woman," Ian

said. "Some of the shit those guys said to her would turn your hair white."

"You're going to turn my hair white, son."

"What did I do now?"

His father turned around and placed his hands flat on the counter, leaning over like he was looking at blueprints.

"I'm trying to see you and her working out," his father said. "I'm afraid I can't quite picture it."

"Don't worry. I can picture it."

"Son, she's a great welder and she works her ass off, but is she really the sort of girl you need to be committing yourself to?"

"Yes."

"You sure about that?"

"Why wouldn't I be sure about it?" Ian demanded. "I like her. She likes me. We enjoy each other's company and you can take that to mean whatever you like."

"Ian, I love you with all my heart. You're my only child and—"

"Here we go." Ian sighed into his coffee. Luckily his father didn't hear him.

"As my only child, I can't help but worry you're getting in over your head here. People who date, who get into serious relationships with each other, need to be compatible. You'd agree with that, wouldn't you?"

"More or less," Ian said. "I know it doesn't look like that on paper, but Flash and I have a lot in common."

"You do? Might I ask what you two have in common? Other than..." He nodded at the condom wrapper on the floor. Ian rolled his eyes and walked over to pick it up and throw it away. Why did he always turn into a teenager around his father?

"Flash is a welder. I work in construction," Ian said. "She likes bar food. I like bar food. She…" Ian struggled to come up with something else, something that didn't involve sex. "Craft beer. We both love craft beer."

"Craft beer? This is something to build a relationship on?"

"Come on, it's Oregon. Half the marriages in this state are thanks to craft beer."

"Probably half the children born, too."

"At least half," Ian said.

"Is she Catholic?"

"No, she says she was raised nothing. But she's very respectful of religion."

"Ian, does she even ski?"

Skiing was the other religion observed in the Asher family.

"No. She's an artist."

"Ah, yes, I remember her telling me that a long time ago. She's good?"

"Incredible."

"And you're such a big art connoisseur you know that she's that good?"

Ian counted to five in his mind. He loved his father. They got along great three hundred and sixty-four days out of the year. Today must be day three hundred and sixty-five.

"Okay, so you have a point. I know nothing about art. But I don't have to know a lot about art to know she's good. She has an installation up at the Morrison this month. That's one of the galleries the Asher Foundation supports, right? If they think she's good, she's gotta be good, right?"

"The Morrison is a reputable gallery, yes. But they

also have a habit of putting on shows by artists who are edgy or offensive just to get the press and more bodies in the door."

"Flash sculpts flowers, Dad. Flowers. Climbing rose-bushes made of aluminum. Eight-foot sunflowers made of copper. I hate to tell you this, but sunflowers are not edgy."

He raised his hands in surrender.

"Forgive me. I just assumed a girl like her was—"

"A girl like what?" Ian asked as he returned to the kitchen and sat back on his stool again.

"A girl with her unique style, I mean."

"Unique? Have you been to Portland recently? She looks like half the women in that town. Which is yet another reason to love Portland." Ian still had his apartment in the Pearl District. He wished he was there right now. "It's not 1965 anymore. Put the cane down, Dad. Stop yelling at kids to get off your lawn."

"So sue me, I'm a little old-fashioned," his father said as he poured a second cup of coffee for himself. "I just remember a time when women looked like women. I assumed my son had similar taste in ladies. Clearly I was wrong."

"Flash looks like a woman. A woman with short hair and a few tattoos. It's not like she's walking around in a snowman costume or a bear suit. Not all women have to look like Miss America contestants. Most women don't."

"It's fine. None of my business," his father said. "You have your fun with her. She seems like the sort of girl you can have fun with. You're still young enough to play around before settling down with someone nice."

Ian should have known this was how his father would

react. He hadn't wanted to admit to himself or to Flash but he should have known...

"I hate to tell you this, but if and when I settle down, it's going to be with her. At least I hope so."

"You're being selfish, Ian."

"Selfish? For dating who I want to date? How the hell is that selfish?"

"Son, nobody knows better than I do how ugly it can get when two people from very different worlds fall in love. Now, I have set you up on dates with some of the classiest, loveliest, nicest and most accomplished women in this state and—"

"Why don't you ask them out if you like them so much?"

"Excuse me?"

"You heard me. You're only fifty-six, Dad. Are you ever going to get married again?"

"Some of us are a little busy running the state and managing *your* inheritance."

"Busy? You take every single January off and spend it in the Mediterranean. Maybe take that month and go out on some dates. I know some of the classiest, loveliest, nicest and most accomplished women in this state, according to you. Although you should know that two out of three of those 'classy' ladies you're so enamored of asked me back to their places on our very first date. So this idea you have in your head that there are two types of women—the girls you 'have fun with' to use your words and girls who are 'nice'—probably needs to go because nice girls like having sex, too. Yes, I am having fun with Flash. I'm also falling in love with her. So if I were you, I'd get used to the idea of having her around, because she's not going anywhere except to every Asher company party, every Asher fundraiser and, as long as things keep going as well as they have been, every single Asher family gathering. I might even talk her into coming to Mass with us on Christmas Eve."

"You do that. I'd love to have her in church with us."

"Is this a photo op for the campaign?" Ian asked.

"No, it's the truth."

"Good to hear it. Now…are we done here? Because if I remember correctly you are here to ski with me, and the more we talk, the less we get to ski."

"We'll go as soon as you're ready."

"Good," Ian said, climbing off his stool. If they were skiing, then they weren't talking about his personal life. Not talking about his personal life was his favorite thing to do with his father.

"Son?" his father said before Ian was halfway to the door.

"Yeah?" He turned around.

"I do like Flash. I want you to know that. I don't want you to think I dislike your girlfriend. I like her very much. You caught me a little off guard. That's all."

"Glad you like her. You should like her," Ian said.

"Your mother…" Dean Asher said, and paused before going on. "Your mother had a very hard time trying to fit in with my family. I wouldn't want someone you love going through anything like that. I wouldn't want you going through that, either."

"Do you regret marrying her?"

His father looked up at him in shock.

"Never. I regret what happened after, yes. But not marrying her. I would never regret that. I have you, after all. Ivy gave me you. And even if she hadn't, even if we'd never had children... No, I wouldn't have regretted marrying her."

"My mother wasn't the sort of woman your parents wanted you to marry, right? Just remember that every time you see me with Flash."

His father nodded.

"I'll remember that. I'll remember that, and I'll try very hard to get used to the idea of having a daughter-in-law named 'Flash.'"

"She also answers to Veronica, you know."

"Veronica. I'll call her that instead. Good Catholic name. Named for Saint Veronica?"

"Named for the girl in the Archie comics."

"I'm going to pretend it was for Saint Veronica."

"You can do that," Ian said. "But you really should go look at Flash's stuff at the Morrison when you get a chance. She's very talented. You'll be impressed."

"I'll make a note of it. In the meantime, I'll stay out of it. You're a grown man."

"Yes, I am."

"Now hurry up and get ready or I'm leaving without you."

"Going," Ian said. He made it two-thirds of the way to the door when his father said his name again.

"Yes, Dad?"

"You weren't kidding? Two out of three of those ladies I set you up with tried to get you back to their places on the first date?"

"Two out of three, and no, I'm not kidding. Disappointed?"

"Very. If they'd gone out with me, it would have been three out of three. You're losing your touch, junior."

Ian laughed all the way to his bedroom. He kept his

mouth shut and didn't tell his father the whole truth—it had been three out of three.

FLASH ALMOST CALLED off her evening plans with Ian. She was so sore from hauling and scrubbing and sanding Ian's heavy iron fireplace screen in her workshop that she almost wanted to sleep more than have sex.

Almost.

But for Ian's sake—and her pussy's—she rallied at about seven o'clock that evening, took a quick shower, threw on clean clothes and drove the thirty miles up the mountain to Ian's chalet.

Chalet? She couldn't believe she was the girlfriend of a man who lived in an actual chalet. The last guy she'd been seriously involved with had lived in more "shack" than "chalet."

She pulled into the long drive that led to Ian's chalet. She spied smoke coming from the metal chimney pipe and felt a sense of comfort at the sight. That chimney smoke signaled that someone was home, someone was awake, someone was waiting for her. And that someone was Ian Asher, who she'd been falling for since the day he showed up at Asher Construction a year and a half ago to take over as the new VP. The rumor had been his father had been prepping him for the role for years, letting him work his way up the ladder at Asher Custom Homes, a smaller residential-only construction firm in Portland. When the former VP had retired, Ian had got the job. She still remembered the day he showed up, gathered the entire crew into the large conference room and introduced himself.

"Yes, the rumors are true," Ian had said, "I am the owner's son. I would apologize, but I'm afraid it would get back to Dad. In case you're worried—and I would be if I were you—I am qualified for this job with something other than my last name. The city of Portland and the surrounding counties are going through a massive growth spurt and people are feeling the growing pains. Rents are going up, and people are being squeezed out. The rest of the country has finally noticed us and they like what they see. So they are coming, and we're going to be ready for them. Asher Construction will be the first call developers make when they want to build sustainable, affordable and beautiful housing, and low-energy, cost-efficient environmentally friendly office buildings. We're going to be part of this city's renaissance, all of us. It takes a talented team of people to build a city. You all build the buildings. I'm here to build the team. Any questions?"

Flash had to stop herself from raising her hand right then and there and saying, "Yeah, I have a question—will you marry me?"

Instead she'd kept that question to herself as she watched Ian introduce himself to every single person at Asher Construction from the foreman of her crew to the two young women who ran the payroll office to the janitor who kept their headquarters clean. When he shook her hand, he said, "So you're the famous Flash Redding? Dad calls you his 'Lady Welder.' Nice to finally put a face with the legend."

She'd been so flustered by his handsome face, his bright and genuine smile, his height and the width of his shoulders that his perfectly tailored suit accentuated so well that when she finally opened her mouth to speak, well…it wasn't good.

"Lady Welder is my porn name," she'd said in reply.

Her very first sentence of greeting to the new boss and it was a stupid dirty joke? She braced herself to get fired on the spot or at least sent to HR for a talking-to. Of all the stupid crass things to say.

"Weird," Ian had said. "Lady Welder's my porn name, too. One of us is going to have to change our name or our fans are going to get very confused. And disappointed." Then he'd given her a little "I'm your boss but I can take a joke" sort of smile and moved on to the person standing next to her.

Eighteen months ago she regarded her feelings as nothing more than a work crush, something to enjoy, something to make work more fun. A harmless crush on an older man with money and power and prestige. It was like having a crush on a celebrity—as playful as it was pointless. Nothing would ever come of it, right? She'd been crushing on the burlesque star Dita Von Teese for four years now and hadn't even gotten one phone call from the woman. Same with Ian Asher, right? A Harvard-educated man commonly referred to in the newspapers as the "scion of the Asher Construction empire" was not the sort of person who dated lady welders. She wasn't even sure what a "scion" was, only that people like her were never called that. Ian was a safe crush. Nothing would ever happen between them no matter how cool she played it, no matter how hard she tried to flirt with him without him noticing, no matter how many times she made him laugh with some sarcastic remark about plumber crack, the scourge of the construction business. No matter how much she wanted it to happen, it wouldn't happen.

And then it happened.

Now eighteen months after Ian started at Asher Construction, she was officially his girlfriend. She should have been on cloud nine with happiness. And she was. One foot was on cloud nine with happiness. The other foot was firmly on the ground, ready to run the second things started turning south.

She pushed her worries into a back corner of her mind as she pulled into Ian's driveway. He saw her coming because he opened the garage door for her and let her pull inside. His own car was outside the garage under a tarp. Bad sign. More snow coming tonight?

When she walked into the house through the garage entrance, she found Ian lying on the floor in the living room flat on his back.

"Help," he said.

"Have you fallen and you can't get up?" she asked, standing over him.

"I fell down a mountain."

"What? You fell down a mountain? Are you okay?"

"Technically it's called 'skiing,' but let's be honest—it's controlled falling. And I did it today for the first time this season. I hurt."

"You went skiing today?"

"Dad made me. And now I can't move. I hate being old. Why am I so old?"

She shook her head in disgust.

"You're thirty-six not ninety-six."

"If you throw yourself down a mountain for eight straight hours, you will feel ninety-six. I don't recommend it."

"Well, I'm only twenty-six and I feel ninety-six."

"Did you ski, too?"

"No, I worked on your fucking fireplace screen all day. It's done, by the way."

"Oh," he said. "Thank you?"

"Don't thank me. Just share the floor. Scoot over."

"I hurt too much to scoot."

Flash put her booted foot on his hip and pushed, sliding Ian two feet to the left.

"I didn't give you splinters, did I?" she asked as she dropped to the floor and stretched out on her back.

"I sanded the shit out of this floor before I refinished it. It is as smooth as Al Green's voice."

"That's pretty smooth."

"It's going to be very hard to fuck you if I can't move," Ian said with a sigh. "And I was really looking forward to fucking you."

"It's okay. We can fuck later."

"I'm going to think about fucking you," he said, and put one hand over his eyes. "That I can do. My brain is the only part of me that doesn't hurt."

"Are you doing it?" she asked.

"Yeah. Totally doing it. Damn, I'm good. I have excellent technique," Ian said.

"Just tell me when I come so I know."

"You're almost there. Almost. Al…most…there… You came. Then I came immediately after. Whew." Ian dropped his hand from his face to his chest. "Wow. I hope it was as good for you as it was for me."

"Better. You fucked me so hard and so good I can't move."

"I'm an animal." Ian made a little growling sound and Flash laughed so hard she groaned from the muscle pain in her back. "Ready for round two?"

"Not yet. I need more time to recover. But I admire your stamina."

"You know what might make us feel better?" Ian asked as he flopped onto his side not unlike a fish on land.

"Morphine?"

"Even better than morphine."

"Heroin?"

"I was thinking more along the lines of something not incredibly dangerous and illegal."

"Vicodin?"

"The hot tub. We could take off all our clothes and get into my hot tub. What do you think?"

"I think I'd rather have the Vicodin."

"You really don't like hot tubs? I thought you were kidding."

"They make me nervous."

"Why do hot tubs make you nervous? If it'll make you feel better, I'll wear my lifeguard whistle and you can put on some of those arm floaty things."

"I'm not nervous I'm going to drown. It's just…"

"What?"

"It's embarrassing."

Ian's eyes widened. "Tell me the embarrassing thing right now. That is an order."

"I got a rash in a hot tub when I was a kid. That's all."

"A rash."

"Yes. A butt rash."

"You got a butt rash from a hot tub when you were a kid. Like…a small rash?"

"Not small."

"Big?"

"Picture a pizza, Ian. That was my twelve-year-old ass."

"Oh, my God! That's so disgusting. I'm never eating pizza again. Don't get me wrong, I'll still eat your ass, but I'm not touching pizza."

"See? You'd be hot tub shy, too, if one turned your ass into a pizza. I couldn't sit for a week. I had to sleep on my stomach. My poor mother had to put the ointment on me. It was a nightmare."

"Where did you get this hot tub butt rash?"

"We went on vacation when I was a kid and stayed at a hotel with a hot tub."

"Okay, hotel hot tub was your first mistake. And your second. One mistake for each ass cheek. Those things are cesspools."

"Now you tell me."

"My hot tub is brand-new, just installed. I cleaned it myself, bleached it twice. The water is perfect. It will not give you a case of pizza butt, I swear."

"You're never going to let me forget about the pizza butt thing, are you?" she asked.

"No. Never. As long as we both shall live."

"Yeah, I thought so. Now you have to tell me something embarrassing." She slowly rolled onto her side to face Ian.

"Something embarrassing? Okay, this isn't as embarrassing as pizza butt, but I could tell you about the time I had sex with my girlfriend and I forgot to get rid of the condom wrapper and my dad found it on the living room floor the next morning."

Flash winced in sympathy.

"Oh, that's bad. When was this? High school?"

"This morning."

Her eyes went wide. "Oh, shit! What did your dad say?"

"He gave me that dad look, you know..." Ian contorted his face into an expression of seriousness mixed with sternness with a dash of trying not to laugh. "Then he asked, 'Anyone I know?' which is a weird thing to say if you think about it."

"Did you tell him it was me?"

"I did."

"Did he freak out?"

"A little at first because he thought you were still an employee. I told him you quit."

"That's all?"

"Mostly," Ian said, shrugging, which she was impressed he could do while lying on his side on a hardwood floor.

"So it wasn't all?"

"He said he had concerns about us dating. The usual dad stuff. No big deal."

"What are the usual concerns?"

"Flash, they're no big deal."

"Tell me what he said."

"Nothing important. He has concerns you'll be uncomfortable with the Asher family when we're being all…" Ian put his finger on the tip of his nose and lifted it.

"Being all important? Being all rich and important? Being all rich and important and doing important people things?"

"Right. But still, this is Portland, not LA or New York. I wanted to remind him we're Ashers, not Rockefellers. We're not even Kardashians. I refrained from saying all that out loud. Barely."

"Your dad has a point."

"No, he doesn't."

"He does. I will be uncomfortable. I am already uncomfortable."

"That's because you're lying on the floor. Get up. We're going to the hot tub. If we're going to have a serious relationship talk we're going to do it naked and in one hundred degree water. Up."

"Do I have to?"

"Yes. I'm the boss. When I say jump you say—"

"Who?"

"Close enough." He rolled over into the push-up position, and with an impressive show of both grace and muscle he jumped to his feet. He reached down and held out his hand. She groaned and let him take her by the arm and drag her to her feet.

"Can you take your clothes off or do I have to undress you, too?" he asked.

"I can undress myself."

"Too bad. I'm going to do it, anyway. Arms up."

"I can't move them."

Ian shook his head. "Pathetic." He took her by the wrists and lifted her arms over her head. Once they were up, he grasped her sweatshirt by the bottom and yanked it up and over her head. Then he unzipped and yanked her jeans down, which was when Flash reminded him that it's usually necessary to take off someone's shoes before you took off that person's jeans. He suggested in the future she invest in skirts preferably with nothing on underneath. She said she'd give that some thought, but considering he lived on top of a fucking mountain with twenty fucking inches of snow on the ground, she'd probably stick to wearing both jeans and underwear. He conceded defeat.

Finally she stood naked—completely—in the middle of Ian's living room.

"You're right," she said, running her bare foot along the hardwood. "This floor is very smooth."

"I'm sorry, I couldn't hear you over the sight of your nipples."

She looked at him through narrowed eyes.

"Ian, stop staring at my tits and take your clothes off."

"I can do both at the same time," he said as he pulled off his long-sleeved black T-shirt and pushed his jeans to the floor. He covered his crotch with his hands.

"What are you doing?" she asked.

"Don't look at it. It's not ready yet."

She threw back her head and laughed. Ian pulled her to him while she was still laughing and kissed her. He had this amazing gift for making her laugh and an even more amazing gift for making her stop laughing on a dime. His kisses were nuclear. They split her open down to her atoms. She melted when he kissed her like this, melted and burned. His tongue tasted like pure heat and his lips whispered words into her mouth, words like "Yes…" and "You want this…" and yes, she did want it. She wanted it all as long as it was coming from him. Slowly he pulled back from the kiss.

"Okay," he whispered against her lips. "Now it's ready."

"Can I look?"

"If you can catch me."

"Catch you?"

Ian darted away from her and to the door that led to the deck and the hot tub. She'd never seen a naked man run so fast. Nor had she ever heard a grown man squeal in that particular high-pitched manner when his feet hit the snow on the deck.

Nothing to do but follow him. As soon as her bare feet hit the deck she knew why he was running and squealing.

"Fuck!" she screamed when her toes touched snow.

"Run, Flash, run!" Ian called to her as he jumped over the side of the hot tub and into the water.

"It's too cold to run."

"Run, anyway!"

"I hate you!" She didn't hate him but yelling it made her feel better. She raced and skidded across the deck to the hot tub and Ian reached out and pulled her over the side and into the water.

She sunk immediately down into the water all the way up to her ears. With her eyes closed she simply let herself absorb the water's heat deep into her body. One by one all her muscles relaxed.

"Do you still hate me?" Ian asked as he wrapped her in his arms and pulled her naked body against his naked body. She twined her legs around his waist, her arms around his neck.

"So fucking much."

She kissed him so he knew she didn't mean it. She shouldn't have worried. His cock was already hard against her stomach. She reached between their bodies and stroked it slowly, exploring every ridge and every vein and every beautiful inch of it.

"Are you having fun down there?" he asked, a wide grin on his face. His words turned to steam as he spoke.

"I am. You're very hard. It's flattering."

"You should be flattered. I don't get stage-three wood in a hot tub very often."

"Stage-three wood? There are stages?"

"There are stages."

"Tell me of these stages while I play. I'm already fascinated," she said as she squeezed him with one hand and cupped his testicles with the other. His mouth fell open slightly and he took a quick breath. Could he be any sexier? It made her weak sometimes. She hated being weak, yet she loved being with Ian so she was either going to have to get rid of Ian or get used to feeling like this all the time.

Ian pressed a soft kiss under her ear. Okay, maybe she could get used to it.

"Stage one," he said. "Flaccid."

"Boring."

"Right? But it's the default position. We like boring in public. If the world made sense men would wear fluffy skirts for boner camouflage and women would wear pants."

"Women do wear pants."

"Someone isn't." He cupped her ass and pinched it.

"What's stage two?"

"Yawning and stretching. You know, like you do when you wake up in the morning, but you're not quite bright-eyed and bushy-tailed yet. That's stage two."

"So stage two is when your cock is awake but it hasn't had its coffee yet?"

"Right."

"So stage three is postcoffee?"

Ian nodded. "Three cups. Wide awake."

"Your cock is wide awake right now?"

"It is ready to take on the world."

"Is there a stage four?"

"Oh, yeah. Stage four is serious business. It's caffeine *and* adrenaline. It's so hopped up it can't sit still. Stage four is usually the last couple of minutes before coming. You know that moment during a shuttle launch when all engines are firing and it's like hovering a couple feet off the platform? That's stage four."

"Is there a stage five?"

"Coming is stage five. There is no stage six. You go immediately from stage five to stage one. Like... in seconds."

"I like stage three," Flash said, running her hand up and down him again in one long stroke. "How long can you stay here?"

"A long time with the proper amount of stimulation. But if it's more than four hours, I have to call my doctor. That's what the commercials say, anyway."

"Am I giving you the proper amount of stimulation?"

"The perfect amount. Absolutely perfect." He put his arms on the side of the hot tub and laid his head back. Flash half sat, half floated on his lap while she played with him, teased him, tenderly caressed him.

"You feel really good," she said.

"You're telling me."

"I mean, you feel good to me," she said, holding him closer, relishing his nearness. "I wanted you for a long time. It's nice to finally be able to have you. I had a crush on you from the day you started."

"You did?"

"I did. Big-time."

He shook his head. "I'm stunned. From the first day?" he asked.

"The very first day. You gave your speech to the company and took the time to talk to every one of us. And you were so handsome. Are handsome. Were handsome. You were then and still are very handsome. And sexy."

"I feel so stupid now," he said. "I'm trying to figure

out a time in the past year and a half when I knew you had feelings for me. I can't. You played it way too cool."

"I did suck your cock and let you fuck me and come on me. That wasn't a hint?"

"I'm trying to remember a time *other* than that night."

"The week before when we were alone at work together? I was practically throwing myself at you," she said. "You didn't get the hint."

"I was close to getting the hint before your stupid ex-boyfriend walked in."

"Oh yeah, Killer. Why did I date that guy again?"

"You tell me," Ian said.

"Before I was trying to stop thinking about you. Didn't work," she said. "My crush on you wasn't budging."

"I thought it was me who had the crush on you," Ian said. "I assumed you slept with me out of curiosity or boredom or, you know, he's here and I'm here so why the hell not?"

"That night was not a 'why the hell not' situation. It was a 'I have to have this man or I will die because my pussy will murder me' situation."

"Did you know I had feelings for you?"

"I knew you were attracted to me. But that's a little different."

"How did you know?" he asked. "I tried not to be obvious about it."

"You have a tell." She tapped the side of her nose, pointed and winked at him.

"A tell? Like a poker tell?"

She nodded.

"What's my tell?"

"When you're working and somebody says something to you, you answer them while you're still working. Unless it's me. You always stopped what you were doing if I said something to you, no matter how minor," she said as she traced circles around the head of his cock with her fingertip. "Steve or Jack or Davis could ask you something while you were reading a contract or blueprints or something, and you'd answer them without looking up. With me you put whatever you were reading down on your desk. Then you looked up."

"I liked looking at you."

"I got that feeling. I liked looking at you, too. You're pretty sexy for a suit," she said.

"You like my suits. Admit it."

"I love your suits. They make you look…powerful, important, in charge. I like a man who wears authority well."

"You like me."

She nodded again, smiling.

Ian grinned that grin again, that "I love my fucking life" grin, which he wore so well. The world had been very kind to him and his one redeeming virtue was that he knew it and appreciated it.

"Since I'm in charge here," he said, "I'm going to give you an order."

"I order you to order me."

"Tell me why you're uncomfortable."

"I'm not. This hot tub is great."

"You know what I mean." He looked at her, grin gone. He was Mr. Serious Ian now. She much preferred Mr. Horny and Distracted Ian.

He put his hand on her face, caressed her cheek.

"Tell me," he said. "You play your cards close to your chest. Let me see some of your cards, okay?"

"It's dumb," she said. "I know it's dumb and you're just going to tell me it's dumb."

"I am not. Tell me."

"You come from a wealthy, powerful and big-deal family and I don't."

"That's dumb."

She splashed water in his face.

"I deserved that," he said.

"You did."

"But it is dumb."

"Ian…"

She moved off his lap and sat next to him.

"I'm only teasing you," he said as he dragged her bodily back into his arms.

"Ian, I have worked at a construction site for two years now. The only woman on a construction crew. I've been called a slut. I've been asked how big my cock is. One guy calls me Lady Gaga all the time."

"No, that's gotta be a compliment."

"Not when the sentence starts with 'Shut the hell up.'"

Ian winced. "I know a lot of the guys felt threatened by you. I'm sorry. I did my best to make it a safe place to work. I know my best wasn't enough."

"It was subcontractors mostly, other guys on other crews who didn't know me and thought they could get away with saying that stuff."

"Can't fire the subcontractors," Ian said. "If they don't work for me, I can't fire them."

"Right. Even if you could, if you fired everyone who

said something inappropriate at work, you would have fired everyone. Myself included."

"That's true. There was the porn name incident."

"Lady Welder is a great porn name."

"Yes, and it's mine. Go get your own."

"Knowing what you know about what my life has been like the past couple of years, do you really think it's irrational of me to be nervous about dating you?" she asked, and waited, wanting a serious answer, needing a serious answer.

Ian gave a heavy sigh and sat up in the hot tub.

"No. It's not irrational. You've had to put up with a lot of shit over the past couple years, and I don't blame you for worrying about having to go through another couple years of proving your worth to people who don't get you."

"Thank you," she said. "I'm glad you understand where I'm coming from. The last guy I dated before you had full-sleeve tattoos and a blue Mohawk. He was a bartender at a music club. We matched. You and I, we don't match very well. We clash. We're like Joe Biden and Joan Jett."

"I can't believe you called me Joe Biden."

"He's the first Catholic guy I could think of who wears suits all the time."

"First of all, Joe Biden and Joan Jett would be the founders of the greatest rock n' roll supergroup ever. And second, we do not clash. You're sexy. I'm sexy. We match."

"You're not listening to me."

"I am. I swear I am. Okay, let's discuss it. Yes, my father has a lot of money and a lot of companies and he's kind of important out there." Ian pointed west toward Portland and presumably the world at large. "But I don't have a lot of money. I make a good salary, but I'm not rich. I own no companies. I'm not important to anyone but my father, my family, my friends and you."

"I know all that. I know you don't care that I don't have much money or that I live in a kind of crappy apartment or any of that. I know." She raised her hands in surrender. "But I also know people aren't going to expect to see someone like me with someone like you. Not even me. When I picture you, Ian Asher—scion of the Asher empire—with somebody, it's not me."

"Who do you picture me with? Is it a guy? Because I picture you with other girls sometimes."

"Ian."

"Is he cute? Is he well-hung? I'm shallow enough to admit that's important."

"Ian."

"Does he like me or is he just using me for sex? I hope he's just using me for sex. I don't want to break his heart, but I'm already in a serious relationship."

Flash had no choice but to sink under the surface of the water in the hopes of drowning. She lasted all of one second under the water before her face nearly melted off from the heat and she resurfaced.

"He is using me for sex, isn't he? I knew it," Ian said with a sigh.

"You are the most annoying man I've ever wanted to have sex with right now," she said, wrapping her arms around his shoulders.

"Too late. I'm stage one again."

"What? That was fast."

"I can't help it," he said with a shrug. "You were talking about my father and it wilted."

She put her feet flat on the hot tub floor and stood up, showing him her naked body dripping with water and illuminated from behind by the deck light.

"That's helping," he said. He reached for her again and she stepped back out of his grasp.

"No touching," she said. "Not until you at least pretend to take me seriously for a few seconds. It's all I ask."

"I'm taking you very seriously," Ian said. "You're my girlfriend and I'm wild about you. I think you're amazing and sexy and amazingly sexy. I want to spend a lot of time getting to know you, hanging out with you, being with you in bed and out of bed. And in hot tub and out of hot tub. Clothed and naked. All of that."

"This sounds very good to me."

"Good. I don't want to be worrying every time we're out in public together that you don't feel like you belong with me just because my father has a lot of money. It's his thing, not my thing. After my mother died, he threw himself into work. He was making millions while I was making those stupid handprint turkeys for Thanksgiving and cardboard Christmas trees covered in cotton balls. Dad's work has nothing to do with me other than he owns the company I work for."

"Don't pretend he's not planning on your taking over the empire."

"He wants that, yes. And he's planning on leaving me his money. But—believe it or not—I love my father. I even like the guy most of the time. I'm really hoping I don't see a penny of the Asher money for decades. I want him to live a very long time and he probably will. My grandfather is still alive, and he's in his late seventies. The Ashers have good genes."

"You move in very different circles than I do. Can you deny that?"

"I go to Dad's corporate functions and campaign fundraisers when he asks me to go. I'd like you to come with me when I go to them but I won't make you. They're boring, but they'll be less boring if you're there."

"You won't feel weird being at some big fancy campaign fundraiser with me on your arm?"

"No. *Weird* is not the word. *Erect* is the word. Which gets us back to the idea of men wearing the fluffy skirts in public."

"I'm picturing you in a poodle skirt. It's very… arousing."

"Speaking of arousing…this is very adorable of you." He waved his finger in a circle in her general direction.

"What?"

"You being nervous about dating me. I've spent the last year and a half being slightly terrified of you. It's nice to know I make you a little nervous, too."

"It's not nervousness. I have pride, Ian."

"Really? I hadn't noticed."

She flicked water at him. It went right up his nose. Score.

"I have pride and I'm not going to take it well if your father's friends treat me differently than they treat you. You understand what I'm saying? I'm not going to stand by silently while your dad's friends talk to you and ignore me."

"Knowing some of Dad's friends they'll ignore me and hit on you."

"Or they'll treat me like shit."

"That's not going to happen."

"It's already happened."

"What? What do you mean?" Ian sat up. Now he was taking her seriously.

"I hate to tell you this, but certain members of your world have made it clear they don't want me in it."

"What do you mean?"

"A couple months ago, I tried coming into your world and I wasn't allowed in. You think I'm making up being worried about us being a couple?"

"What are you talking about? When do you try to come into my world?"

"Two months ago, I tried to come to the twenty-fifth anniversary party for Asher Construction."

He narrowed his eyes at her.

"You didn't come to the party. I was there."

"I said I 'tried' to come. I didn't make it inside."

"Chicken out?" He wouldn't blame her if she did. In October, his father had thrown an anniversary celebration at Portland's most elegant hotel. It was a black-tie affair and everyone from the mayor of Portland to the coach of the Portland Timbers came. Everyone who worked full-time for Asher Construction had been invited but with the invitation stressing the requirement of formal attire, almost none of the rank-and-file workers had shown up. He'd hoped Flash would show up. He would have given half his salary to see her in a cocktail dress. All night he kept one eye on the door and one eye on whoever he was trying to have a conversation with. But Flash never showed.

"I don't chicken out," she said. "I came. I came in a dress, a gorgeous dress Mrs. Scheinberg had lent me. Red, strapless and stunning. I had black elbow gloves. I had my hair professionally done so I looked like a red-headed Twiggy with tattoos. And I showed up at the front door looking like a million dollars and then some. And they wouldn't let me in."

"What?"

"You heard me. Security wouldn't let me in since I hadn't RSVPed in time. I told them I worked for Asher Construction on the crew. The guy laughed and said, 'As what?' I told him I was a welder. He laughed again and said, 'Sure thing, honey. Nice ink, but the Ashers don't like crashers.' He was pretty proud of himself for that one."

"Fuck."

"I tried to get him to find your father. I asked for Mr. Asher and some guy came over and said I should probably run along before they had to call the police."

"Did this man kind of look like Gene Hackman?"

"Yeah, kind of. Had the mean eyes."

"That's my dad's ex-campaign manager, Jimmie Russell. He's kind of an asshole."

"I noticed. He and that security guard looked at my tattoos and my piercings and my hair and decided I wasn't good enough to be in the same room as you and your family. He told me to run along back to my strip club because my pole was waiting for me."

"He said what?"

"You heard me," Flash said. "And you want to know the really wild thing?"

"Probably not, but tell me."

"That dress Mrs. Scheinberg lent me was vintage Givenchy. It cost thousands of dollars when Dr. Scheinberg bought it for Mrs. Scheinberg in 1960. It's worth a fortune now. I was dressed better than him, your father and you combined."

"You didn't deserve that," Ian whispered, true words but they didn't seem like enough.

"Nobody does."

"Men like Russell don't know something valuable when they see it. But I do."

"Are you sure about that?"

"I spent that entire four-hour party watching the door, hoping you'd show up. I got cornered by one of dad's friends trying to talk me into investing in some scheme of his. That must have been when you tried to get in."

"I didn't care about the party. I only went there to tell you I was sorry for what I'd said when you dumped me. And maybe make you a little sorry you'd dumped me. Then they kicked me out. Not much humiliates me, Ian, but that was humiliating. I cried in Mrs. Scheinberg's apartment when I gave her the dress back."

"Jesus Christ…"

"I don't think you can say that anymore, now that we know you're Jewish. But I'm not sure. We'll have to check the bylaws."

He laughed and groaned at the same time.

"Ian?" she asked. "You okay?"

He shook his head.

"No? You aren't okay?" she asked.

He looked up from the cradle of his hands and smiled.

"I hate everything forever," he said. "On earth. Right now. This second."

"Welcome to my life."

"I told Dad I thought the black-tie anniversary party was a waste of money and a bad idea. I said we should have a company barbecue. Something everyone could come to without feeling like they had to drop a ton of money on formal attire. He said every Asher event was a campaign fundraiser whether we wanted it to be or not. Fat cats don't go on picnics, and we needed the fat cats on our side. I lose a lot of these arguments."

"I'm glad you tried, though," she said.

Ian leaned his head back against the edge of the hot tub and exhaled so hard a whole cloud of smoke billowed from his mouth and nose and up into the night sky.

"I feel like I'm always apologizing to you," he said. "And here I'm doing it again. I'm sorry. That was a horrible thing to do to you and say to you and I would have put Russell in the hospital if I'd known what was going on."

"I know it wasn't your fault. I know you would have let me in the party. It's not you. It's just…nobody wants to see the captain of the football team with the weird Goth girl at school. They want to see him with the head cheerleader. I'm not a cheerleader, Ian. I eat cheerleaders."

"Literally or in a sexual way?"

"Both," she said. "I'm a bisexual cannibal and proud of it."

"You're wrong, by the way."

"About what?" she demanded. "I'm never wrong."

"About the football captain and the weird Goth girl. You said nobody wants to see them together. I want to see them together."

"What about your grandparents? What about your dad's business partners? What about your friends?"

"I don't care. I don't care. I don't care. And they shouldn't, either."

"What if your grandmother says something to you about my tattoos?"

"Never too early for the old folks' home, Grandma."

"Oh, my God, you're ridiculous. Can you not be serious for three seconds?"

"I can't help it," he said with that grin again, that gorgeous grin. "I'm too happy." He put his hands on her waist and gently drew him to her.

"You're cute when you're happy," she said. "Why are you so happy?"

"Because two days ago I thought you were walking out of my life—forever. And now you're my girlfriend. Why wouldn't I be happy? I'm stoned to the gills on hormones. Aren't you?"

"Stoned?"

"Happy?"

"I'm—" she settled onto his lap again, straddling his thighs and resting her chin on his shoulder "—cautiously optimistic."

"It's a good start." He kissed her cheek, her forehead, her lips. "I want you to be happy, though. You make me very happy."

"I know I do," she said, and pushed her hips into his erection. He was back at stage three again.

"Not that kind of happy. I mean, also that kind of happy. But also the regular nonerect kind of happy. My dream girl now my girlfriend. Why wouldn't I be happy?"

Flash raised her eyebrow?

"I'm your dream girl? Really?"

"Apparently I have a thing for women with ink, short hair and very bad attitudes. Maybe it's an opposites attract thing. Maybe it's a fetish. I don't know and I don't care, but you're the sexiest woman on earth, you're terrifyingly talented and you get me off like nobody's business. And you're also nearly impossible to read, impossible to please and impossible to impress. So when I do read you, please you or impress you, it means something. I like that you make me work harder than I usually have to," he said. "Most women smile all the time because they're told they're supposed to smile. I love that you don't smile except when you mean it. When I make you smile I feel like I won a contest—first prize."

Flash smiled.

He cupped her chin in his hand. "Yeah, just like that. I'm a winner."

"What should I give you for a prize?" she asked.

"You," he said. "You're all I want."

"Then you can have me."

He took her in his arms and turned her, pressing her back to the side of the hot tub. Her legs were wrapped around his hips and his arms around her lower back. He lifted her up so that her breasts were out of the water, and as soon as the cold winter's night air touched her skin, her nipples hardened. Ian lowered his head and licked the water off the center of her chest. His took both her breasts in his hands and lightly squeezed them as his tongue tickled the sensitive skin of her neck and chest. She was warm from the waist down and covered in delicious goose bumps from the waist up. When he took one of her nipples in his hot mouth, she flinched from the shock of pleasure. Her breasts were so sensitive in the cool air and every touch and every lick she felt all the way to her back and down into her hips. Weightless as she was in the water, it was easy to lie back with her legs around Ian and her back arched to the sky as he sucked her nipples and rolled his tongue around them. First one, then the other, then back again. Over and over he lavished them with attention with his mouth and his tongue. He caught her mouth in a sudden hard kiss. He cupped her with his large hands again, squeezing them harder this time, pinching her nipples, rolling them between his fingers and thumbs while she moaned into his mouth. His cock was brutally hard against her thigh. She wanted it inside her so much her pussy throbbed.

"I need to be inside you," he said, pressing his chest to her breasts. She loved his chest, his hard flat stomach. She would never get enough of his body.

"Then come inside me."

"Can I?"

"You know you can."

"You know what I mean." He licked her from the tip of her shoulder to her ear, nibbling her sensitive skin with his teeth. "You're my girlfriend now. We're committed. I want to act like it."

"You want to come in me."

"Will you let me?"

"Have you been tested recently?" she asked, putting her hands on his shoulders. She needed breathing room.

"Yes. You?"

"Right after we slept together," she said. Ian raised his eyebrow at her. "What? Don't take it personally. You can't be too careful."

"I'll try not to. What do you say?"

"You're in charge," she said.

"Not with something like this. You tell me."

Having sex without a condom was serious relationship business. She had an IUD and wasn't worried about getting pregnant. And if Ian was okay and she knew she was...

"If it's too soon," he said, "no pressure. It's just, condoms and hot tubs don't really mix. Not that I've tried."

"You've tried," she said. Ian nodded. "Is that why you want to?"

"No," he said. "That's not why."

"Why?"

"You never make anything easy, do you?"

"No, I don't. Tell me why."

Ian rested his forehead against hers. His hands held her by the waist. They were so close they were breathing the same air.

"Because I want to, because I want to be closer to you, because I want you to feel like I'm serious about being with you. And because I don't want anything standing between us and you seem to think there is. I promise, nothing's going to come between us except what you want between us."

Flash shivered and it wasn't from the cool night air.

"I don't want anything between us," she said. She lifted her wet hands and slicked his hair back from his face. She wanted to see his eyes. They were burning blue like the hottest part of a flame. His lips were slightly parted. He was breathing hard and so was she.

"Neither do I. But if it's too soon—"

"It's not too soon."

"Because if it is too soon—"

"I'm in love with you, Ian, and I have been for a long time. It's not too soon."

Ian's eyes flashed with surprise.

"You're what?"

"I'm in love with you and I have been for a long time."

"How long?" He sounded so surprised she almost laughed except now wasn't the time for that. "I know you said you wanted me from the day I started at work, but that's not…that's not love."

"Since that night in June. Six months. That's why—"

"That's why it hurt you so much when I had to break it off with you."

"That's why," she said. "I had a crush on you at work, that's all. You were sexy and I liked you, wanted you. But I didn't let myself have strong feelings for you until that night. I hadn't planned on it. I wasn't gunning for you. I never thought in a million years anything would really happen with us other than work flirting. We went back to your place and we had crazy sex and then you asked me to spend the night, which I didn't expect. I woke up at about 4:00 am and thought I should probably just sneak out. I tried and you woke up and caught me. You remember?"

"I remember."

"And you pulled me back into bed with you and you kissed me senseless and then you got on top of me and got inside me again and when you pushed in you said my name. You said—"

"Veronica."

She closed her eyes and remembered that moment he entered her, the way her name had fallen from his lips like he'd been holding his breath, and when he exhaled, it was her name that he breathed. He'd never said her name before—only Flash, never Veronica. She'd forgotten he'd known her real name and then to hear him say it in that breathless desperate way while he was penetrating her, it was like he'd cut her open all the way to her heart.

"The way you said it like it was a magic word or something, like you were asking me for something or begging me for something or praying for something, but it got to me. It was just about sex before then. And when you said my name, my real name, then it was real."

"It was real," Ian said. "It was the most real night I'd ever spent with anyone."

"I'm telling you this because you said you didn't want anything between us. Now that I've told you there's one less thing between us."

Ian ran his hands up and down her sides, over her breasts, over her chest, over her neck and up to her face.

"Veronica…" he whispered.

"I'm here."

"I wasn't saying it to you," he said. "I was saying it for me."

"I love you, Ian."

"Flash—"

"I want you to take me to bed and do everything you want to do to me," she said. "And I don't want anything between us. Okay?"

Ian kissed her forehead and it hurt almost as much as when he called her by her name.

"Okay, Veronica. Nothing between us. Not ever again."

9

FLASH WAITED IN the hot tub while Ian found towels for them both. She nearly screamed in shock when her hot bare foot touched ice cold snow, but she managed to make it into the house without passing out from sudden-onset hypothermia. Ian toweled himself off quickly and roughly, then wrapped the towel around his waist. Then he helped her dry off, rubbing the soft white towel up and down her naked legs while she dried her hair. When they were in the house again, warm and mostly dry, he kissed her once on the lips and said, "I have to cover the tub and turn it off. You go up to my bed and warm up. I'll be there soon."

"Anything you say, boss," she said as she pulled the towel tight around her and headed up to his third-floor bedroom.

She sat on the edge of his bed and waited. It made her smile to see that he'd lit the first and second candle in his menorah earlier this evening. The flame had gone out but she could tell from the solidified white wax that he'd let them burn a long time. Ian was a good man. Only a good man would light that candle because lighting that candle honored both her, since she'd made the menorah, and his mother, since that was who Flash had made it for. She hadn't been here at sunset. Ian had done it alone, on his own initiative. It meant everything to her that he'd lit that candle. She wasn't even Jewish, and she felt blessed by it.

And now he knew she was in love with him. She couldn't quite believe she'd told him. She hadn't planned to tell him, not unless or until he'd told her first. But she could tell it hadn't been easy for him to ask if he could be inside her without a condom. He'd taken a risk by doing that. She couldn't let him be the only person in this relationship willing to take a risk. Now she'd done it. He hadn't said he loved her back and that was fine. She didn't want him to, not yet, not until she was sure she'd believe him when he said it. But she knew it was okay. He'd been surprised to learn she loved him but not angry or apologetic. She didn't need him to say it back to her, not when he said her name like that.

"Veronica?"

Yes, just like that.

She looked up and saw Ian standing in the doorway, still wearing the towel wrapped around his waist.

"I'm here," she said. He stepped into the dark room illuminated by nothing but the little bit of moonlight reflecting off the snow in the evergreen branches.

"You warm yet?" He stepped in front of her and she leaned against him, her cheek against his stomach.

"Getting there. This helps," she said as he ran his hands all over her back and shoulders.

"What else would help?" he asked as he ran one hand through her hair, slicking it back. She'd never dated a guy who had the same length hair she did. Maybe they could go to the same barber. The thought made her smile. Ian made her smile. She smiled now as he took his towel off and tossed it to the corner of the room.

"That helps," she said, looking up at him. "That definitely helps."

"What about this?" He moved to stand between her knees, nudging her thighs apart with his legs. Then he dropped to his knees and pulled her hips to the edge of the bed.

"Warmer," she said.

He kissed her neck.

"Warmer..." She sighed.

He licked her right nipple.

"Warmer..."

He sucked her nipple into his mouth, gently but deeply.

"Very warm..."

He pressed a long kiss onto her quivering stomach. Then he turned his attention to her left hip where he bit into her lightly and sucked her skin for a long time. When he pulled back he'd left a love bite the size of a quarter on her body.

"Marking my territory," he said. She held on to his shoulders as he did it again on her right hip and again on the soft underside of her left breast. He left another red and purple bite on her chest under her collarbone and a last one on her right thigh as big as two quarters. The bites hurt and she loved it, loved to watch him leave imprints of his mouth all over her.

"How warm are you now?" he asked.

"Not warm," she said. "Hot."

"Hot is good. Burning up is better." He pushed her onto her back and dragged her legs over his shoulders.

He opened her up with his fingers, spreading her folds wide. He licked her slowly from the base of her vagina to her clitoris and Flash shivered and moaned. He did it again, even slower this time, even deeper. She could feel her body opening up to him, growing wet inside, growing hotter. She needed him inside her—the sooner, the better.

"Ian?"

"Yes?" He flicked his tongue over her clitoris again.

"Could you do me one little favor?" she asked.

"Name it."

"Put your cock inside me."

She saw his eyebrow twitch.

"Say 'please and thank you' and I'll consider it."

"You're going to make me beg?"

"No. I'm going to make you ask for my cock very nicely. Like a lady."

"I won't do it." Flash Redding did not beg for cock.

"Fine. I'll just be down here eating your beautiful pussy until you learn some manners."

He spread her wider and pushed his tongue inside her again. He licked her and licked her and licked her until she was writhing on the bed under his mouth, unable to lay still, unable to stay silent. He'd bring her close to orgasm and then back off by pausing to kiss her thighs and hips again. When her heavy breaths softened he started again, lapping at her clitoris and all around it until she was in agony from the need to come.

And still Ian wouldn't let her orgasm. As her whole body clenched, right at the edge of climax, Ian pulled back again.

"Well?" he asked from between her thighs. "Do you have anything to say to me?"

"Will you please put your cock in me?" Then she added a second "please" for good measure.

"I will. But only because you asked nicely." He took her legs off his shoulders and stood up. He was fully erect again—halfway between stage three and stage four. Good to see she wasn't the only one about ready to burst around here.

"Get back on the bed," he said as he stood up. She scooted back and started to turn over onto her stomach. "No, on your back."

She looked over her shoulder at him. He crawled across the bed to her. They'd never had sex with her on her back before, always on her stomach or on her hands and knees or like last night, bent over at the waist with her leaning against the wall. He liked entering her from behind and she liked it, too, for the simple reason it made her feel dirtier.

Slowly she eased down onto her back as Ian knelt between her open thighs.

"Still cold?" he asked as he stroked her thigh with his fingertips.

"No. Burning up."

"You're shivering."

"You made me almost come three times and pulled back. You're lucky I haven't passed out yet."

"If you'd minded your manners I wouldn't have had to teach you a lesson. I run a tight ship around here. No insubordination allowed."

"I'll be good from now on," she said. "Lesson learned."

"That's what I like to hear. I don't ask for perfection, just improvement."

He lay on top of her and she wrapped her arms around his neck.

"I like you," she said.

"I know. You told me that in the hot tub."

"I told you I loved you. I didn't tell you I liked you."

"You told me two days ago you didn't like me."

"You've grown on me."

Ian smiled as he settled in on top of her. Flash opened her legs and lifted her hips for him.

"I like that you like me," he said. "I like that almost as much as I like that you love me. I like you, too." He reached between their bodies and notched the tip of his cock at the entrance of her body, but didn't go in yet. "Can you tell?"

She nodded slowly, panting, "I can tell."

He rocked his hips, his cock sliding through her swollen folds. Still he didn't enter her. He seemed intent on dragging this out as long as possible, delaying the inevitable. He was torturing her, and she loved it.

She moved with him, lifting her hips against him. He was as hard as she was wet. The muscles in her back knitted up with the sweet terrible tension. Ian put his hands on either side of her and rose up over her so that only their pelvises were touching. He rocked his hips again, another time, a third.

"Ian?"

"Yeah?"

"Please?"

He looked in her eyes without smiling, without speaking. Intense eye contact in bed usually made her a little nervous. It did now, too, except it also made her ache in the sweetest ways. This was real, her relationship with Ian. It was real and serious and was about to get much more serious. He tilted his hips and pushed the tip inside her. She inhaled and grasped the sheets between her fingers. Slowly he slid all the way in, filling her, stretching her, opening her, taking her, having her.

"Veronica..." He whispered her name as he penetrated her fully. When he was in, all the way, so was she. In lust, in love and in for good.

He lowered himself on top of her again, stretching out on her—face to face, chest to chest, hips to hips, eye to eye.

"How does it feel?" she asked as he pumped his hips again.

"Incredible."

"Tell me," she said. "Please? You made me do it."

"You really want to know what your pussy feels like on my cock?"

"Yes."

"That's asking a lot of a man when his cock is inside your pussy."

"You made me do it," she repeated. He laughed softly.

"True. It's, ah...hard to explain. The first couple of thrusts are the best, especially if you've been hard for a long time before going in, like I have been all night. It makes your eyes roll back in your head, which I know isn't sexy, but fuck, it feels so good you can't help it."

"It is sexy when you do it. I like seeing you enjoy my body."

"You have no idea how much I enjoy your body. You're really wet right now and hot. A hot wet pussy sort of feels like that soft smooth part of your mouth right inside of your cheek. You know, except tighter and there's no teeth."

"Tighter?"

"You're clenching me again. I can really feel it. It's not quite like being squeezed by a hand but sort of. You have this one muscle that I can feel when your pussy contracts. It's like a finger squeezing instead of a whole hand." He held up his hand and crooked his finger to demonstrate.

She concentrated and clenched her vaginal muscles around him. Ian flinched.

"Yes," he said. "Just like that. And…" He paused to catch his breath. "It kind of feels like you're pulling me in deeper when you do that."

"I am."

"It's literally the sexiest feeling in the world when you do that because it's like your vagina can't get enough of my cock, and just needs more and more of it, deeper and deeper."

"It does, Ian.

"Your pussy feels so good with nothing between us. If I cry when I come inside you, just pretend you don't see it."

"See what? I don't see anything."

"That's my good girl."

He pumped his hips again and Flash lay back underneath him with her eyes closed and let it all wash over her. His thrusts were hard but steady, deep and forceful, but not painful. He knew exactly how to fuck her the way she needed and wanted. Her vagina pulsed around him, muscles twitched in pleasure, her breath hitched in her throat and her chest. Ian's body was hot on top of hers. They were both sweating and the wetness made it all the sexier. The bed creaked underneath them and nothing, not even a bomb going off outside the house, could have stopped them in this moment. She couldn't stop moving, couldn't stop writhing. She felt so open and wide and slick and Ian pounded into her with thrusts that took her breath away. She could have lain there taking it for days, it felt so good. She hooked her feet over the backs of his muscular thighs and clutched his shoulders in her hands, wanting to be as close to him as possible. Every thrust into her sent pleasure shooting from her hips to her nipples and all the way into the backs of her thighs. This was full-body fucking, nothing held back from either of them. Sounds escaped her lips—moans and gasps, groans and cries. She couldn't get enough of his cock, of his body, of his thrusts, of him.

When she lifted her hips into him, he grazed her swollen clitoris, and when he pulled out her pussy ached to be filled again. The next thrust into her met that desperate need and the cycle started all over. She was wild underneath him, pumping her hips in rhythm with his thrusts, her breasts swollen with desire and her nipples hard as diamonds. It was a thousand degrees in the room, a million. She needed air but they couldn't stop. They'd die if they did. She was so close to coming, so close it hurt. Ian must have sensed it in her movements or her breathing. He shifted his weight onto his knees, held her by the waist and slammed into her, impaling her as she came and came, every muscle inside her body spasming and contracting and releasing only to contract again even harder, clutching at his cock and squeezing it. She felt a rush of wet heat inside her as Ian came with her and inside her and with her name on his lips.

Ian collapsed on top of her and she lay limp and spent

beneath him, her pussy still fluttering around him with final tiny contractions.

"Are you crying?" she asked.

"No."

"Are you lying?"

He laughed softly. She loved feeling his chest moving against hers. They were so close she could feel his laugh even better than she could hear it.

"Maybe." He turned his head and she looked at him. No tears.

"That was the best orgasm I've ever had," she said. "I thought you should know that."

"The best?"

"Top five at least."

"I'd run a victory lap right now but my cock's still in you."

"Still hard?"

"No, but I think I'm stuck. You have a pussy like a steel trap."

Flash rolled her eyes and opened her legs wide. Ian slid out of her and rolled onto his side. They lay facing each other. The moon shone through a break in the tree cover and white light filled the room, enough to see each other by, and enough for Flash to see a dozen red bruises on her breasts, stomach, hips and thighs.

"I can't believe you gave me hickies," she said. "They're all over me."

"Really? You can't believe that? It really seems like something I would do. Because it is. Except..."

"What?"

"I think I missed a spot when I was marking my territory."

"Do not put a hickey on my pussy."

"I don't know if that would work, but I wouldn't mind trying. Hold still."

"Ian…"

He pushed her onto her back and she braced herself for whatever he was about to do to her. He slid on top of her and pressed his mouth to her chest and left a small bite right over her heart.

"There," he said. "Perfect."

"Can I mark my territory, too?" she asked.

"No."

"Why not?" she demanded.

"Because you'd have to mark every square inch of me," he said.

Flash stared at him through narrowed eyes.

"Challenge accepted."

Flash jumped on top of him and started biting.

IAN WOKE UP around midnight and instinctively reached over to Flash's side of the bed. It was empty.

"Fuck."

"Already?"

Ian smiled and sat up. Flash stood in the doorway to his bedroom.

"Where'd you go?" he asked. She was fully dressed— jeans, boots, coat, everything.

"Nowhere. Yet."

"Are you leaving?"

"We are," she said. "Get up and get dressed."

Ian eyed her suspiciously.

"Where are you taking me?"

"You'll see," she said. "I think you'll like it."

"I don't know about this." Ian threw the covers off him and started gathering his clothes. "It's midnight and you're being mysterious. This is the beginning of a horror film."

"It is."

"I knew it. You're going to murder me and dismember my body, aren't you?"

"Would I do something like that?" she asked.

"Probably," Ian said.

"You may have a point there." She walked over to the bed while he was tugging his socks on. She bent and kissed him on the mouth. "I promise, I'm not going to murder you and dismember your body tonight. Now hurry up. I'll meet you downstairs."

"Thank you. Wait. What do you mean you won't murder me 'tonight?'" he called out as she walked out of the room. "Does that mean you won't murder me ever or you just won't murder me tonight?"

Flash didn't answer.

He finished dressing and went downstairs. She handed him his heavy winter coat and gloves.

"Are you going to tell me where we're going now?" He pulled on his gloves while she yanked her red wool toque down over her ears.

"Out," she said. "Out there." Flash pointed at the patio door.

"Into the woods?" Ian pulled his gray beanie on and down over his ears.

Flash opened the back door and stepped out onto the deck.

"You coming?"

"Fine. I'm coming." Ian closed the door behind them and followed her down the deck steps and onto the snowy path. "But if a bear or a wolf shows up, I'm letting them eat you while I run away since this was your idea."

"I accept your terms. Now hold my hand, dammit."

"Okay, dammit," he said, taking her hand in his. They trudged through the crunching snow, stumbling over twigs and rocks buried under the white powder. They passed under tree branches thick with snow and ice and scrambled over fallen tree trunks festooned with deep green moss. They worked their way up the hill toward a clearing in the woods. It was slow going in the snow and the cold and walking uphill. Although they'd walked half an hour, they hadn't traveled far enough to even lose sight of the chalet roof half a mile behind them. They reached the clearing where the tree line thinned and met the edge of a heavy snowpack. His nose was red and running, his eyes were lined with tears and his lungs burned from the thin air and the uphill walk.

And yet...

Above them the full moon glowed bright as the daytime sun and the snow all around them shimmered like white marble and quartz. Away from the city the stars came out—millions of stars, billions of stars, more stars than God could count. Flash was smiling and Ian forgot all about the stars.

"Damn, it's beautiful out here," Ian said, squeezing Flash's gloved hand in his. "I'm glad we came out."

"I said something mean to you," she said.

"I probably deserved it."

"You didn't deserve it when I said I only wanted to use you for sex. And you didn't deserve it when I said I didn't want to hold your hand and go walking in a winter wonderland with you."

"Is that why we're out here?"

"I thought it would be a better way to say 'I'm sorry' than just saying 'I'm sorry.' I do want to hold your hand. I do want to go walking in the snow with you. I want us to have a real relationship. I love having sex with you but I do want more than that."

"I want that, too," Ian said. "I'm ten years older than you are so it's only right that I warn you that I'll want to get married sooner rather than later. I think I even want a kid—one at least, two at the most. Those things are important to me. And if you can't see that happening with me—"

"I can," she said.

"You can?"

"Yeah. With you I can see that happening. It scares me but in the good way, the way I get scared when I get a good idea for a sculpture and I don't know if I can pull it off or not but I have to try."

"This feels real, what you and I are doing," he said. "I need it to be real. I don't want to dick around. I don't want to screw this up. I want the real thing with you and I want it now. We've waited long enough to get serious with each other."

"I feel the same way," she said. "It's a relief to hear you say it."

"How would you feel about me giving you the key to my place?" he asked. "That way it won't be breaking and entering when you wait outside the bathroom while I'm in the shower."

"I think I like that idea."

"What do you think about moving in with me up here?" Ian tensed. He knew he was pushing things with her but right now with the snow under their feet and the stars over their heads like an umbrella, he felt like he could say anything to her.

"Are you in love with me?" she asked.

"You know I am."

"Say it."

"I'm in love with you, Veronica Redding. I am deeply in love with you. I spent the last six months trying not to be in love with you, and there were days when it was physically painful to be around you and not tell you what I feel. It felt like I had a vise clamped on my heart and now it's finally off. All the pain in my chest is gone. I know it's kind of soon to mention all this, but I've spent six months not being able to take a full breath because of you and now I can breathe again and all I want to breathe in or out is you."

There was that smile again, that smile as rare and lovely as a rose blooming in winter.

"I can't move in with you," she said. "I want to. I do. But I can't afford it."

He laughed. "You think I'd charge you rent? I don't want or need your money."

"Yes, but I want and need my dignity. I'm not going to mooch off you just because you can afford it."

"But—"

"I can't," she said again. "And I swear, it's not you. I've been in love with you a long time. You asking me to move in with you feels like Santa Claus showed up and asked me if I wanted a new Lincoln Electric torch kit and two tons of scrap metal. Of course I want it. But I'm not sleeping with Santa Claus. I can't take charity from the man I'm in love with. I love it when you play the boss when we're in bed together, but when we're not in bed, I need us to be equals. I can't be in your debt."

"I get that, I do," he said. "When I was in my twenties, I lived in a whole series of shitty apartments because I wouldn't take money from Dad, and I didn't want to live at home. But you already told me you're going to be making the same amount at Clover's nursery as you were at Asher. Does that mean we're never going to live together?"

She sighed and blew a cloud of smoke all the way up to the moon.

"How about this?" she said. "How about we wait until I sell a sculpture? I only have to sell one and I can afford to pay my fair share of this place for at least a year. Then I can move in and not feel like a gold digger."

"I only make two-fifty a year. It's more like a bronze digger."

She laughed. "You know what I mean."

"I know what you mean. Okay, it's a deal. I don't want to wait but I can. For you I can definitely wait."

"The Morrison Gallery is doing a big show and a nightly gallery hop the week before and on Christmas. I might sell something. You never know."

"And then you'll move in with me?"

"And then I'll move in with you."

"You promise?"

"I swear."

"And you said I can't buy one of your sculptures?"

She shook her head. "No cheating."

"Fine. No cheating."

With her hand in his, he started to pull her back toward the path, back toward the house. He couldn't wait to get her into bed again and make love to her until morning.

"Wait," she said. "Look."

She pointed at the sky and Ian followed her finger to

where what appeared to be a small meteor was streaking through the cluster of stars and toward the horizon.

"Make a wish," she said.

Ian made his wish.

"What did you wish for?" Flash asked.

"For you to sell a sculpture."

She laughed softly. "You want me to move in that much?"

"I want you to be happy," he said. "And I know that would make you happy."

He looked at her and saw tears rimming the edges of her eyes. They glowed white in the moonlight.

"You're trying to get me into bed, aren't you?" she asked.

"Is it working?"

"It's definitely…" Flash took a step back. Her eyes went wide. Too wide.

"What?"

"Ian," she whispered. "There is a giant fucking bear behind you."

"Shit, what?" He whipped his head around and saw nothing, absolutely nothing.

Then he heard footsteps running in the snow.

And laughter. So much evil laughter.

"Made you look!" Flash called back.

"You are in so much trouble!" he yelled, and started chasing after her.

He heard Flash laughing all the way back to the house.

10

Ian took off work early on Friday the eighteenth for the very good reason anyone takes off work early on the Friday before Christmas week—because he could, because there was nothing else to do at work since it was the week before Christmas and because he wanted to have sex with his girlfriend—the sooner, the better.

He hadn't been to Flash's apartment yet and that was for good reasons, too—Flash hadn't asked him over, and he was still working on his house every free moment he had. But work had taken him into Portland, past Flash's apartment complex, and as they'd been officially dating and sleeping together for two weeks now, he figured he'd earned the right to show up unannounced at his girlfriend's place to surprise her with flowers and the erection he'd been trying to keep subdued the past hour—all Flash's fault. In general the bulk of his erections were her fault simply by existing but this one was undeniably all her doing. An hour ago he'd texted her asking if she wanted to get dinner at the Timber Ridge Lodge tonight. She'd said she would as long as they could also get a hotel room and have sex with her tied to the bed. He'd agreed and discovered he couldn't get a hotel room until tomorrow night, which he'd promptly booked. With that image she'd planted in his head, there was no fucking way he could wait the twenty-four hours to make that fantasy come true. He could only hope she was home and in a bondage sort of mood. He'd brought her flowers. If that didn't do the trick, he had no idea what would, but he was willing to try begging.

He pulled into her apartment parking lot shortly after five. The complex was nice if somewhat bland. All the buildings looked the same, but they were well-made housing blocks with nicer-than-average landscaping. The abundance of elevators and wheelchair ramps attested to the complex's past life as a retirement complex. Flash had said her downstairs neighbor was in her late eighties. Perhaps she was a holdout from the old days.

With his flowers in hand he walked up the stairs to Flash's door and knocked. There was no answer. That was surprising as she hadn't said anything about going into town today. He knocked again and waited. Nothing. He sent her a quick text asking her where she was. She replied a few seconds later with a terse Driving.

Well, shit.

He put the flowers outside her door. As quiet and well-managed as the place seemed, he didn't think the flowers were at risk of being stolen. He walked back down the stairs and was on the last step when a door behind him opened.

"Veronica, is that you?"

Ian looked around and found a white-haired woman in a pale blue wool dress standing in a doorway.

"Not Veronica," he said. "I was just looking for her. She went out, I guess."

"She did," the elderly woman said. "I thought she'd come home and I'd missed her. I need her help with something."

"Can I help you?" Ian asked. "I'm her boyfriend."

The older woman smiled and her eyes sparkled with mischief.

"Ian Asher. I should have recognized you. Your hair's gotten too long. Would you like me to cut it for you? I always cut my boys' hair."

"Thank you but that's okay. I'm getting it cut tomorrow."

"Oh, yes, the Christmas party is Sunday, isn't it? You do have to look nice for that. Your father's announcing his reelection campaign, isn't he?"

Ian grinned. This woman knew his life better than he did.

"You have to be Mrs. Scheinberg," Ian said. "Flash told me about you."

"And she's told me quite a bit about you. Come in, come in. She should be back soon."

"Do you know where she went?"

"She's been cleaning out her workshop all day now that she's done with her sculpture."

"She's done already?"

"Oh, yes, took it to the Morrison two days ago. They wanted it there in time for the holiday gallery hop tonight. Here, let me take your coat."

Ian shrugged out of his coat and passed it to her. She hung it in the hall closet. She had a nice place. Very old-fashioned but elegant, just like she was.

"I can't believe she finished it that fast. I need to go see it."

"You should. She showed me a photograph. Just exquisite. She said she was inspired," Mrs. Scheinberg said with an impish twinkle in her eyes. "And a little happiness helps with the creation process. I never believed that old yarn that artists have to be miserable to make art. I know Veronica. She does her best work when she's happy. And you have made her a very happy lady this month. Sit. I'll make tea."

She pointed at the kitchen table chair and Ian sat as he was instructed. He would have offered to help but she seemed completely capable of making tea on her own.

"Thanks for letting me wait here for her," Ian said. "Any idea when she'll be back?"

"Soon, I imagine. She's been gone awhile and she said something about being back in time for dinner with you. You've been very good about planning dates, I've noticed," Mrs. Scheinberg said as she put water in her tea maker. "My husband was a planner, too. Very thoughtful. Always planning something fun for us to do together. He's been gone ten years, but I still have over fifty years of good memories to keep me company until we meet again."

"Sounds like he was a great husband."

"The very best. But you'll make a good husband someday, too. I can tell." She gave him a little wink as she carried two mugs of tea over to the table.

"You can tell? Good. I'm glad someone can. When I was a kid, I thought by the time I was thirty-six I'd already be married and have kids of my own. I was fifteen years old when my father was my age. I'm running a little behind."

She waved her hand dismissively.

"Times are changing, Mr. Asher. People live longer. What's the rush settling down? You settle down when you meet the right person, not because you think it's the right time. You hadn't met the right person yet. Now you have."

Ian smiled behind his tea mug.

"Now I have," he said.

"That's good to hear. My son is insisting I move in with him and his wife. He says he can't sleep at night thinking about me all alone. I tell him I'm not alone, that I have my Veronica one floor above me. He says Veronica can't always be there. So…he's right about that. This is proof. My light bulb is out in the bathroom and I can't stand on the chair to change it. And where's Veronica? Not here."

"I'm here."

"But you won't always be here, either. And as long as she has you and she's happy, I can be happy and move in with my son without worrying about her being alone. She's not alone anymore so I can go."

"I'm sure she'll really miss you."

"She will. But she can come see me anytime she wants. I'll have my own little house in his backyard. They call it a 'mother-in-law suite.' Isn't that something. A whole house to keep the mother-in-law out from underfoot but close enough to keep me out of trouble."

"I've built a few of those," Ian admitted. "We call them guesthouses, though. It's a little less insulting."

"I'm not insulted. I like my daughter-in-law better than my son most days. She has a sense of humor at least. She has to have one to be married to him. But you know something about that, dating my Veronica. She's what we always called a 'tough cookie.'"

"She's a tough cookie, all right. I must like tough cookies."

"Smart men do," Mrs. Scheinberg said, nodding her approval. "Would you like a cookie? I have frosted Christmas cookies."

"No, thank you. Wait, Christmas cookies? I thought Flash said—"

"Oh, yes, I'm Jewish. But I'm a sucker for a frosted Christmas tree. Veronica sneaks them to me. She's my dealer."

"She's a good one," Ian said.

"The very best." Mrs. Scheinberg sat her cup down on the table. "Now that I've had my tea, would you do me the favor of changing my bathroom light bulb? I may need to see in there very soon."

"It's my pleasure."

She took him to the bathroom where he quickly replaced the light bulb.

"You're very tall," she said. "I'd have to stand on a chair and my balance isn't what it used to be. Another reason to move in with my son. Do you know him? Moshe Scheinberg?"

"Heard of him. Hospital administrator, yes?"

"That's him. He knows your father. Donated to his campaign."

"Well, thank your son for us. I'm sure Dad will be hitting him up again soon."

"We'll be ready," she said. "Are you looking forward to the Christmas party?"

"I'm not dreading it. Can't say I'm excited about it."

"You should be excited. Veronica will be wearing my

red Givenchy. I'm making her wear it. Second time's a charm, yes?"

Ian grimaced. He'd forgotten Flash had told her neighbor about the party incident.

"About that," Ian said. "I still feel terrible. But I promise, nothing bad is going to happen at the Christmas party. I'll be with her."

"Good. They call people like Veronica 'crabby' but that only means she's got a hard shell. Inside she's soft as the rest of us. She takes things much harder than she lets on. She was very hurt that night. Very hurt. It's been good to see her so happy lately. She says her new sculpture is the best work she's ever done."

"I hope it sells fast," he said.

"She does, too."

Ian grinned. "I'll tell you a secret. I asked Flash to move in with me."

"You did? She didn't tell me. When is she moving?"

"She's not. Not yet. She said she can't move in with me until she can afford to pay her half of my monthly mortgage payment."

"You have to respect that woman."

"I do, although she drives me crazy with her pride."

"Let me ask you these three questions, Ian Asher. First, would you want to date a woman without any pride or self-respect? Second, would you want to date a woman who expected you to foot every bill? And third, would you want to be with a woman who was attracted to you *because* of your father's money or attracted to you *in spite* of your family's money?"

He gave her a rueful smile. "Yeah, you may have a point there."

He started to ask Mrs. Scheinberg a question but he

heard the familiar sound of a pickup truck door opening and slamming shut.

"That's her," Mrs. Scheinberg said.

"I should go. Thank you for the tea."

"You're welcome, dear. Thank you for taking good care of Veronica. She's been a dear friend to me and I have very few dear friends left."

"I'll be your dear friend, too, if you like," Ian said.

"That would make me very happy." She patted his cheek. "Such a handsome boy. But you need to cut your hair."

"Tomorrow morning," he said again. "I promise."

"Good boy. Now go on. She'll be happy to see you."

Ian took his coat out of the hall closet and noticed the Givenchy dress hanging in a clear plastic dry cleaner bag. He looked at it and he looked at Mrs. Scheinberg.

"Can I ask you something strange?" Ian asked.

"Strange questions are my favorite questions. Go on."

"Are you really, *really* attached to this dress?" he asked.

"My husband gave it to me, but I haven't worn it in forty years. Middle-aged spread is a menace to the waistline, young man."

"Are you planning on giving it to anyone?"

"I haven't thought about it. Everything I own goes to my two sons in my will. I don't think either Moshe or Michael will wear it. Not their color. Why do you ask?"

"Because I need to get Flash a Christmas present, something special."

"Red is her color," Mrs. Scheinberg said.

Ian smiled.

"Yes. Yes, it is."

FIVE MINUTES LATER Ian knocked on Flash's door.

"Who is it?" she called through the door.

"Joe Biden."

The door flew wide open and Flash stood there in the doorway.

"You're not Joe Biden." She started to shut the door but he put his foot in to stop it.

"I'm a Catholic dude in a suit. Close enough, right?" he asked.

She looked him up and down.

"Close enough."

"You got my flowers?"

"I did."

"Did they please you?"

"I was pleased," she said.

"Did they please you enough that you'll allow me to have my manly way with you?" he asked.

"I'll consider it. Come in." She stepped back and let him in. Before she could even lock the door he pulled her to him and kissed her.

"Ian, stop," she said, pushing him away. "I'm disgusting."

"You're a little foul-mouthed, but hardly disgusting."

"Let me take a shower before you manhandle me," she said. "I smell like a blacksmith fucked a coal miner in an oil refinery."

"Mmm…the sweet, sweet scent of fossil fuels…" He pressed his nose against her neck and inhaled.

"I'm covered in grease and brass polish and you're going to get it all over your suit."

"Don't care. Got lots of suits."

He pushed her up against the wall and kissed her. She laughed and surrendered to him as he knew she would.

"You look incredibly sexy right now," he said into her ear as he pulled up the bottom of her T-shirt and touched the bare skin of her stomach. She was wearing ripped jeans, her steel-toed work boots, a tight white T-shirt covered in grease stains. Her arms were dirty, too, and she had a streak of something black across her cheek. Her hair was sweaty and disheveled, and she smelled of sweat and metal polish. "I think I have to fuck you. What do you think?"

"I think I've heard worse ideas. But I've heard better ideas."

"What's a better idea?"

"Fucking me *after* I take a shower."

"Terrible idea. This is exactly how I want you," he said, sliding his hands up her back to find the clasp of her bra. "This is how you looked after work every day."

"Disgusting? Dirty? Sweaty? Gross?"

"Hot. Hot. Hot. So…" He unhooked her bra. "Fucking." He lifted her shirt off over her head. "Hot." He slid her bra down her arms and tossed it onto the floor. His mouth found her mouth and kissed the life out of it as he took her breasts in his hands and massaged them.

He was rock hard already and there was nothing for it but to bury himself inside his unbearably sexy girlfriend as soon as humanly possible. Nothing would stop him from dragging her jeans and panties down her legs, tearing them off, unzipping his pants and fucking her right here against the front door. Nothing. Not an earthquake, not a volcano eruption, not the end of the fucking world.

"Mreow."

"What was that?" Ian asked.

"My pussy," Flash said.

Ian looked down at her crotch.

"What's it trying to tell me?"

"I need to feed my pussy."

"Is that what we're calling it now?" he asked. "Because I'm into that."

"Oh, my God, I have to feed my cat. Excuse me." She patted his erection. "You excuse me, too."

She grabbed her T-shirt off the floor and pulled it on. A small striped gray cat sat in the doorway to the little kitchenette.

"Ian, this is Bob Ross. Bob Ross, this is Ian. You two make friends," Flash said as she went into the kitchen and picked up a bowl from the floor.

"Why is your cat named Bob Ross?"

"He's my favorite artist obviously."

"Your favorite artist is the happy little tree guy?"

"And happy clouds," Flash said. "You can call him Bob if you want. Or Ross. Or Bob Ross. He's a cat so he answers to none of them."

"Hello, Bob Ross," Ian said. "You are cock-blocking me. Do you know that?"

Bob Ross only looked up at him and blinked. It was a disdainful blink.

"Can I pet you or will you bite me?" Ian asked Bob Ross.

"Only one way to find out," Flash said as she opened a cabinet.

"Is he a biter?"

"No more so than I am."

"Not comforting," he said, remembering the dozens of love bites Flash had left all over his body two weeks ago.

Ian held out his hand and Bob Ross sniffed it be-

fore sauntering in the kitchen without giving him another look.

"I think he likes me," Ian said.

Flash only smiled as she put the cat food on the floor
in front of Bob Ross.

"That should keep him busy a couple minutes," she
said. "How fast can you fuck me?"

"Pretty fast," he said. "Is there a need for speed
here?"

"He'll get on the bed with us and make us pet him.
Very hard to fuck and pet a cat at the same time. I've
tried."

"Can't we just not...pet him?"

Flash looked at him as if he'd asked if they could
skin Bob Ross and eat him for dinner.

"Okay, can't we shut the door?" he asked.

"He'll whine and caterwaul until we let him in."

"Can we fuck in the shower?"

"I hate shower sex. The stall's too small."

"All right. A quickie, it is, then," Ian said, ripping
his tie off. "Let's do this."

"Goddamn that was sexy.".

"What was?" he asked. "Tell me so I can do it again."

"Ripping your tie off like that. That was insanely
sexy." Flash put her hands on his chest and made as if
she wanted to tear his shirt off him. "I've seen you in
ties and out of ties but that was the first time I've ever
seen you tear yours off. Please do it more often."

"You want me to put it back on and do it again?"

"After," she said. She glanced back over her shoulder at Bob Ross still eating. "We have to hurry. Bob
Ross eats fast."

"I'm hurrying. I'm hurrying." Ian grabbed Flash

around the waist and hoisted her squirming and screaming self over his shoulder.

"Ian!"

"What? You said we had to hurry."

"Mrs. Scheinberg is going to think I'm getting murdered up here."

"She knows I'm here. We've met." Ian strode down the narrow hallway to Flash's bedroom and threw her down onto her back on the bed. "Even if she calls the cops, I'll be done by the time they get here."

"I might not be," she said. He looked down at her and raised his eyebrow. Two nights ago she'd come before he was even inside her. This woman could orgasm easier than he could most nights.

"Okay," she said. "I'll probably be done."

"Thought so."

She unzipped her jeans and he yanked them down her legs. He opened his suit trousers and pulled his cock out. They were on a deadline here. No time to disrobe entirely. He climbed on top of her and pushed her legs wide with his knees. Underneath him, she arched her back, grinding her pussy up and down his cock.

"Are you going to tie me to the bed?" she asked as he lifted her shirt to kiss her breasts. He pulled back and looked down at her.

"Look—you can have bondage or you can have a quickie. But you can't have both at the same time. Also, you don't have a headboard so I'd have to install brackets to tie you to the bed."

"I wouldn't do brackets. You could damage the drywall." She tapped the wall. "Maybe a tension rod, floor to ceiling like a stripper pole?"

"With a tile ceiling?" He shook his head. "Wouldn't

hold. Plus you wouldn't screw the brackets directly into the wall. You screw two-by-fours into the studs and then install the brackets into the two-by-fours. Minimal drywall damage."

She nodded. "I hadn't thought of that."

"It's how I mounted the flat screen on the wall at my place."

"Good idea. Until then we can use the rope that's under my bed," she said.

"You have rope under your...never mind. Not asking. Stay."

She stayed. He pulled an eight-foot length of black rope out from under the bed.

"Suggestions?" he asked.

"Loop it around the bed leg."

"Genius." He looped it around the leg and pulled it up to the mattress, grabbed Flash by her wrists and tied them together with a neat camping knot he hadn't used since his Boy Scout days. "How's that?"

"Pretty good," she said, testing the ropes, and they held her arms fast to the bed above her head. "But now I want to try mounting bondage brackets into my wall."

"You can later. I'm mounting you first."

"If you—"

He entered her with one hard deep thrust.

"Insist," she gasped as her eyes closed with pleasure and opened again with desire.

Ian laughed softly and kissed her throat with warm wet nibbling kisses, her favorite kind.

"I insist," he said into her ear, and she shivered all around him. They were panting already, so eager for sex that foreplay went flying right out the window. Flash put her heels into the mattress and lifted her hips, riding his cock from below him. He watched her face as he fucked her, watched her pupils dilate, watched her pale cheeks flush and her eyelids grow heavy. He loved watching her while he was inside her. There was no better show on earth. When he thrust in, her head tilted back, baring her throat to him. When he pulled back to the tip, she lifted her head as if seeking him out. In again and her eyelashes fluttered, her lips parted and she moaned.

He set a steady pace—not too fast, not too slow— and pumped into her warm wet hole. Moments like this he imagined he could spend the rest of his life inside this woman. A lock of sweat-streaked red hair fell over her eyes and he pushed it out of the way for her since her hands were tied. She turned her head into his hand and kissed his palm. His pushed his thumb into her mouth and she sucked on it while he increased the pressure, pounding into her until the bed moaned as loudly as she did.

He pushed her T-shirt up to her neck again, baring her breasts. He latched on to her right nipple and sucked deeply and possessively. Her body was his, all his... It was so easy to play at being her boss in bed and out of bed, but there was no denying it—he was entirely in her power, under her spell and her command. But she wanted him to be in charge, so he took charge as a gift to her and because her submission was a gift to him that it gave her pleasure to give. He would have told her all of that if he could have, but his heart pounded wildly in his chest, his lungs burned, his thighs burned and everything burned all because of her.

"Ian..." She said his name for no reason and he didn't ask what she wanted, because he knew what she wanted—him. So that's what he gave her.

He wrapped his arms around her body, clutching her to his chest as he rode her with his final thrusts. He wasn't going to last much longer and neither was she. He could already feel her vagina clenching around his cock, squeezing and releasing, pulling and contracting.

"Come when I come," he ordered. "Not until then."

She nodded, too breathless to speak. He loved trying to control her orgasms. It was like trying to tame a tiger in that it was nearly impossible and would probably get him killed one of these days.

But what a way to go...

Ian dug his hand into her hair, cradling the back of her head, forcing her to meet his eyes. With their gazes locked on to each other, he lengthened his thrusts as she tilted her hips to meet every last one of them. It was all heat where they joined and unbearably delicious tension. He gave and he gave and she took and she took. She let out a little sound, a cry almost like pain, and he knew she couldn't hold back anymore. Neither could he.

"Now, Veronica," he said as he finally let go of his self-control. His come shot out of him in hard spurts deep inside her while she came all around him, shuddering and shivering with a loud cry that died on her lips and turned into the faintest weary gasp.

He sunk down on top of her, relaxing completely as she wrapped her naked legs around his back, holding him to her and in her.

"I am crazy about you," he panted. "If you hadn't noticed."

"I noticed," she said breathlessly.

"Good. Very good." With a groan he rolled off her and onto his back. It was then that two things happened at once. A ball of gray fur landed on his face and someone knocked loudly at the door.

"Veronica, dear? Are you all right?" came Mrs. Scheinberg's voice through the door. Another series of nervous knocks followed. "Veronica—I heard screaming."

"Told you so," Flash said with a sigh.

"That's it. You're moving in with me," he said as he quickly untied her hands, cleaned his semen off her and tossed her the panties he found under the bed.

"Is that an order?" She looked back over her shoulder at him. She was naked from the waist down and her pussy was dripping with his come. It was the sexiest thing he'd ever seen in his life. Therefore he answered her in the only way his heart and cock would allow him to answer that question.

"Yes. That's an order."

"And I have to obey it?'

"Absolutely. You have no choice."

She pulled her underwear on, dragged on her jeans with a little hop step and ran her hands through her hair.

"No," she said, and walked out of the bedroom to deal with Mrs. Scheinberg.

"Okay, take your time. Think it over."

Ian rolled onto his side and came face-to-face with Bob Ross and his big green eyes.

"Hey," Ian said. "What's up?'

Bob Ross turned onto his back, four paws dangling in the air.

"So…we should get to know each other. We're going to be roommates someday."

Bob Ross looked up sharply as if he'd heard a noise.

"Yeah, I know she said she's not moving in with me, but she'll change her mind, right?"

Bob Ross looked dubious. Then again, didn't all cats always look a little dubious?

"Be straight with me, Bob Ross. You know her pretty well," Ian said. "What do you think I should do to get her to agree to move in with me?"

Bob Ross turned onto his side and started licking his own crotch.

Ian nodded, impressed by the cat's understanding of the situation.

"Good thinking."

Flash came back into the room and stood in the doorway with her arms crossed over her chest.

"Mrs. Scheinberg has a message for you," Flash said.

"What's the message?"

"She says, 'Well done.'"

Ian crossed his legs at the ankles and threaded his fingers together behind his head.

"I aim to please."

"She thought we were fucking, but she also sort of thought you were stabbing me to death."

"Not my fault you're a screamer."

"If you hadn't been here, I wouldn't have been screaming. Therefore it's your fault."

"No, it's your fault for living here when you could live with me."

"Ian."

"I'm just saying you should move in with me."

"I'm not opposed to it. I even like the idea. But."

"But. I know, not until you sell a sculpture."

"Right. And you need to accept that might take a while."

"Or…you can move in with me right now and just pay your part of the rent in sex. Barter system, right?"

"That's the worst idea I've ever heard."

"You're the one who tried to trade welding services for my body two weeks ago!"

"Oh, yeah, I did do that, didn't I? But no, I'm not moving in with you until I sell a sculpture. Case closed."

"Case open. I know how to convince you. Bob Ross told me how."

She looked at Bob Ross and then back at him.

"And what, pray tell, is that?"

Ian grabbed her around the waist and threw her onto the bed. He wriggled her out of her jeans and underwear again and buried her head between her legs.

"Well," she said with a happy sigh. "Bob Ross does have a point there."

Ian opened her folds and licked her still-swollen clitoris. Bob Ross was curled up on Flash's pillow and contentedly purring. Mrs. Scheinberg knew no one was getting murdered. Nothing was going to stop them now.

Flash's phone beeped.

"Ignore it," Ian said between licks.

"I'm ignoring it."

The phone rang this time. Flash sat up. Ian groaned and rolled onto his back.

"Hold your tongue," Flash said, picking up her phone off the side table. "It'll just be a minute. It's the gallery. Hey, Vaughn," she said when she answered the phone. "What's up?"

While Flash was on the phone Ian got into a staring contest with Bob Ross. He won but only because Bob Ross fell asleep halfway through the game. Whatever Flash was talking about with the gallery owner, it must be important. She pulled on her underwear and walked out of the bedroom, the phone tucked between her ear and her shoulder. The call went on long enough Ian started to worry. Finally Flash came back into the bedroom and sat on the edge of the bed by her nightstand.

"What's going on?" Ian asked as Flash carefully placed her phone back on the charger. She moved slowly, deliberately, as if she'd been stunned. "Bad news?"

"No." She shook her head. Her eyes looked glazed.

"Baby, what's wrong?" he asked, sitting up and taking her in his arms. She leaned against him, her forehead on his shoulder.

"My sculptures."

"What? What happened? Was there a fire? A flood? What?"

"Vaughn, the owner, he says someone came in and really liked my stuff."

"That's good. Who?"

"He couldn't tell me. Some rich art collector. But he loved everything I did. Especially my new piece. And then…"

Ian grabbed her by the shoulders and looked her in the face.

"And what?"

"He bought one. The one I did of your mother. He bought it—for twenty thousand dollars. Oh, my God… Ian."

He took her face in his hands, kissed her and kissed her. She was crying so hard with happiness she could barely kiss him back. His heart nearly burst with love and pride. This woman, this incredible woman with dozens of burn scars and old cuts all over her body from spending the last ten years of her life devoting her every single free hour to learning to weld and sculpt and create flower gardens of iron and copper and steel. Had any woman ever deserved success more than this one?

"You're amazing," he said. "I knew someone would see how good you were. I knew it. We have to celebrate. We have to celebrate like crazy. We need to call, like, everybody. You probably want to call your mom. And Mrs. Scheinberg. Bob Ross, are you freaking out, too?"

Bob Ross released a little wheezing cat snore. Flash laughed so hard she snorted again.

"Okay, forget Bob Ross. He's a cat," Ian said. "What does he know about art? No offense," he said to Bob Ross, who was looking very offended at the moment. "Are you freaking out? I'm freaking out."

"I'm freaking out." She put her hands on her head and spiked her sweaty hair straight up.

"You look like you've been electrocuted." Ian spiked his hair up in solidarity.

"I feel like it."

He pulled her to him in a hug and rocked her while she cried in her happiness. He kissed her head, her neck, her cheek.

"You know what this means, right?" she asked.

"Yeah, it means you're buying dinner. And it means you're the real deal. I already knew that but I'm glad everyone else will know it now, too."

"Well, all that. But this means I can move in with you," she said. She wore the biggest smile he'd ever seen in his life. He was blinded by the joy and yet he couldn't look away from it.

"Yeah, if you want. I mean, I want. I really want. But I won't make you just because you sold a sculpture. I only want you to move in with me if you want to."

"I want to."

"Are you sure?"

"I'm sure. I'm absolutely sure," she said. "I've never been more sure about anything."

Flash kissed him again and Ian pushed her onto her back, deepening the kiss until they were both red-cheeked, breathless, wild.

"We have to celebrate," he said. "We have to."

"What do you suggest?"

"I'm going to do what I was doing before we were rudely interrupted by all of your dreams coming true." Ian pushed her legs wide. "I'm going to eat your pussy."

Bob Ross sat up like a shot and ran straight out of the room.

Ian called out after the terrified cat, "The other pussy!"

11

FLASH DRESSED FOR the Asher Christmas party and, at Mrs. Scheinberg's request, let her neighbor do both her hair and her makeup.

"Easy on the lipstick," Flash said as Mrs. Scheinberg applied the lip liner. "I usually don't wear much."

"You will tonight. Bright red. You'll look glamorous. Even better, you'll look like Christmas."

"You don't even celebrate Christmas," Flash reminded her.

"Ah, but I do celebrate glamour. There. All done. Go look at yourself."

Flash walked to the mirror on the back of Mrs. Scheinberg's door and nodded her approval. She felt like Holly Golightly in Mrs. Scheinberg's sleek red dress with the fitted square neck and her black elbow gloves and high heels.

"Wow. I do look glamorous. I don't look like me, but I look good."

"You look beautiful. Just like you. Do you like your hair?"

Mrs. Scheinberg had curled it with a fat curling iron,

and after adding a little hair gel, Flash had a head full of sleek and elegant waves.

"It's perfect. Thank you for everything," Flash said, and left a bright red kiss on Mrs. Scheinberg's cheek.

"My pleasure. Now you need to go. You'll be late."

"I'm going. I'll have the dress back to you by tomorrow night," Flash said.

But Mrs. Scheinberg only smiled.

"No rush. Kiss that handsome man of yours for me when you see him."

Flash grinned. She'd been doing that a lot lately.

"My pleasure."

She headed for the door.

"Veronica, dear?"

"Yes?" Flash turned around.

"A little birdie told me that Mr. Ian Asher has a big present he's giving you tonight."

"Is he?" Flash said, smiling again. "That devil. It's not even Christmas yet."

"He is. I want you to know that you should accept this gift even if you don't want to at first."

"You're being strange."

"I know," Mrs. Scheinberg whispered. "But I'm eighty-eight so I get to use that as my excuse. Now go. Have fun. Be safe."

Flash had no idea what big gift Ian was giving her tonight. The mystery occupied her mind the entire ride to the Mount Tabor neighborhood of Portland. Ian had warned her a week ago that he would have to meet her at the party. His father would need him to help organize the staff and that was Ian's job every year. Flash didn't mind. It would give her a second chance to make her grand entrance and blow Ian's mind. He'd never seen her in a dress before, not even a skirt. All she wanted to do was put a huge smile on his too-handsome face, kiss him, drink wine together and celebrate their first Christmas together. The first of many, she hoped.

And tomorrow, she'd put in her thirty days' notice on her apartment and start moving her stuff into Ian's house.

"Oh, shit," she breathed when she pulled up to Ian's father's house. She knew it would be a nice house. Dean Asher was a millionaire, after all, but she hadn't expected this place—a sprawling white Victorian mansion that consumed the large corner lot it had been built upon. White Christmas lights edged the roof, the porch and the balcony, and their yellow glow made the whole house look as if it had been trimmed in gold leaf. Every door wore a green-and-red wreath and every window held a flickering yellow candle. And through the front bay window Flash spied a Christmas tree that must have been twelve feet tall from the looks of it. And Ian wondered why sometimes she worried he was out of her league...

Then again, maybe there were some perks to dating a rich guy's son. This was a nice fucking house. Spending Christmases here would not be a chore. When she imagined herself growing up in a house like this, she couldn't imagine she would have turned out as well as Ian did. Ian was down to earth, normal, grounded. He didn't throw his money around. He could have lived in a house like this in a wealthy neighborhood and he didn't. He could have driven a Porsche but instead he drove a Subaru like everyone else in Oregon. And he could have fallen in love with someone with money or connections. Instead he'd fallen in love with her. If he wasn't going to punish her for being working class, she wasn't going to punish him for belonging to the one percent as long as he didn't lord his father's money over her. And so far he hadn't. So far he'd been the perfect boyfriend. Although he had apparently gotten her a big Christmas gift. That made her a little uncomfortable. She hoped it wasn't expensive whatever it was.

Flash tried not to think about it. She was nervous enough as it was, coming to this important Asher family party. Ian said all his dad's family would be there— aunts and uncles and cousins and second cousins and grandparents. She'd find one of the out-of-town cousins to talk to, preferably one who felt as out of place as she did. They could hide in the corner somewhere, sip wine and ignore the rest of the party.

As she pulled in front of the house she saw that Ian's father had hired valets to park the guests' cars. Valets? For a private house party? Flash took a deep steadying breath. She could do this. She was an artist, after all. A real one now that her work had sold to an art collector. When people asked her what she did for a living she could say with all honesty, "I'm a professional artist." She'd been waiting for years to be able to say those words. She told herself she didn't care what Ian or anybody was giving her for Christmas this year. Some stranger out there with good taste and deep pockets had already made her biggest dream come true. What more could she ask for? Nothing.

She passed her keys to the teenage valet who declared, "Cool truck," before hopping in and driving it away. She really hoped Dean Asher had hired those guys. If you wanted to make good money stealing cars, this crowd was the one to target. She walked through the front door of the house—no one stopped her—and found a glittering horde of people gathered in the downstairs rooms. She saw the mayor, the governor, a few cast members from that TV show that filmed in Portland every summer and drove Ian crazy by blocking traffic in front of his Pearl District apartment. Everyone was dressed to the nines. Some to the tens. Like that guy over there in the tuxedo and the white bow tie who could have been James Bond, as suave as he looked in that getup. She stared at him boldly, and he returned the stare before plucking a champagne flute off a passing tray and walking over to her where she stood under a large bough of mistletoe hanging from the ached doorway.

"Did it hurt?" he asked.

"Did what hurt?" she replied as she took the champagne from his hand.

"When you fell from heaven?"

"Ian—that was the most pathetic pickup line I've ever heard. And I've heard a lot of them."

"I'll have you know that was a very good pickup line."

"Was it?"

"You're going to have sex with me later, right?" he asked.

"Well…yeah."

"Then clearly it worked." Ian bent and kissed her lightly on the lips. She wanted more of a kiss than that but she saw a flash when their lips met—someone in a suit had just taken their picture.

"What was that?" she asked as the man in the suit with the camera slipped into another room.

"Reporter from the *Portland Mercury*," Ian said as

if she should have known. "Drink up, we need to go meet the fam. Also, you look incredible." He held out his arm and together they walked from the front room down a hall toward the sound of voices coming from a back room.

"You don't look so bad yourself. I'm glad you like the dress."

"I love the dress. I love the lady in the dress even more. And I will love the lady out of the dress most of all."

"You're already trying to get me naked?" she asked.

"Yes. My old bedroom's upstairs," he said. "We will make a pilgrimage to it before this night is over."

"Is that an order?"

"Yes."

"Just in case I never told you," she said, standing on her tiptoes to whisper in her ear. "I love your orders."

Ian kissed her again in the darkened hallway before leading her through the door. He'd brought her to a large ebony wood paneled library where young women in red and silver sequined dresses sat on the arms of leather sofas chatting to men in tuxedos. An older couple sat on the sofa with a baby between them kicking her feet in shiny new baby girl shoes.

The chitchat quieted as Ian cleared his throat.

"Everybody, I want you to meet Flash, my girlfriend. Real name Veronica, everybody calls her Flash. She's a metal sculptor and a welder and the best thing that's ever happened to me. So be nice or you're all out of the will."

"Whose will?" asked a girl who was obviously a teenager and trying very hard not to look like it tonight.

"Yours or Uncle Dean's? Because I'll behave for Uncle Dean's will. Probably not yours, though."

"That's fair," Ian said. "Flash, this is my cousin Angie. Angie, Flash."

"Hi, Flash. Cool ink," Angie said with a bright smile, and Flash thanked her very sincerely. So far tonight she'd had her truck and her tattoos complimented. She might survive this party, after all.

She met Ian's grandparents, John and Marianne, and the baby was Penny, his cousin Jake's daughter. The introductions rolled on for a few minutes until she was dizzy with names, relations and connections. But so far so good. Everyone was friendly, especially Ian's grandparents.

Her tension started to ease as she fell into comfortable conversation with Ian's aunt Lacey and her daughter Petra. They talked about Portland's art scene, a topic Flash could handle with ease. Petra was an aspiring writer who was heading into an MFA program in the fall. Flash talked about the handful of art classes she'd taken, and when she casually mentioned she'd sold a piece recently, Petra high-fived her. She had a novel on submission and knew what it was like waiting for that all-important phone call.

"How you doing?" Ian whispered into her ear as they walked to the large formal living room for his father's announcement. Flash braced herself for more photographs.

"Good. I like your family."

"They like you."

"They're drunk," she said. "Of course they like me."

"There are benefits to being in a Catholic family," he said.

"You have three uncles and four aunts and that's just on your dad's side of the family."

"There are downsides to being in a Catholic family."

"I'm never going to remember all their names."

"Don't worry about that," Ian said under his breath. "I don't even remember them."

"I heard that," Ian's uncle...Lewis? said. Yeah, Lewis. Maybe. Or Louis. Oh, fuck it. She was buying them all name tags for Christmas.

The family lined up along the walls of the elegantly appointed formal living room as Ian's father stood in front the Christmas tree as several reporters took pictures.

"You have a reason for inviting us?" one reporter asked Dean Asher. "Or did you just miss us?"

"I missed you, Joe. You have no idea how much I've missed having you at my house. When was the last time?"

"Four years ago," Joe the reporter said. "Last time you announced you were running for the senate."

"You're stealing my thunder," Dean said.

"So that means you are running for reelection?"

"No," Dean Asher said.

"No?" Joe said. Everyone in the room went silent. This was not the announcement everyone had been expecting.

"Instead I'm running for the House of Representatives. You know, the big one. In DC."

"Oh, holy shit," Ian breathed. The entire room heard.

"Thank you for that, son," Dean Asher said. "My first endorsement, everyone."

With that, everyone in the room applauded and

cheered wildly. Under the cover of the noise, Ian leaned in and whispered in her ear.

"Second floor," he said. "Last room on the left."

"What is?" she whispered back.

"My old bedroom. Slip out while nobody's watching us. I'll be there in fifteen minutes."

"You're really going to fuck me at your family's Christmas party?"

"Do you even have to ask?"

"You know, Mrs. Scheinberg said you had a big Christmas present you were going to give me tonight. Is it your cock?"

"I can't tell you that. It would ruin the surprise."

"Okay, I'm going," she said. "But if you show up with your dick in a box, it's not going to be a happy holiday."

Flash slipped out of the living room while Ian's father was launching into a speech about why he was ready to go to Washington. She didn't feel too bad about missing out on the speech. First of all, Ian had ordered her to go upstairs. And second, Dean Asher already had her vote. Not like she was going to vote against her boyfriend's dad.

Trying to look as casual as possible, Flash headed up the stairs with a purposeful stride. If anyone saw her and wondered where she was going, she'd simply tell them she was looking for the bathroom. Too much champagne. That excuse worked every time. She made it to the second floor and found it much cozier and homier than the downstairs. No fancy oil paintings on the walls up here. No leather sofas and libraries that looked like something out of an English manor house in one of those mystery movies where the murder is always solved by the unassuming old lady. She peeked in on one room and found a simple yellow guest bedroom. Another room was nothing but labeled file boxes— years and years of tax returns for all of Dean Asher's business ventures. Boring. She couldn't wait to see Ian's childhood bedroom. She hoped it was full of embarrassing stuff like photographs of him at prom or posters for stupid movies he'd been obsessed with as a kid or old *Playboy*s or something good. Something she could tease him about mercilessly for as long as they lived.

She opened the door and flipped on the light switch.

Her heart fell to her stomach and stayed there.

Standing right in the very center of the floor of Ian's old bedroom was a sculpture. Her sculpture. The sculpture he'd inspired her to make while talking about his mother.

"You son of a bitch," she said, choking back tears. Ian did the one thing she told him not to do. He was the one who bought her sculpture from the gallery. This was supposed to be the amazing Christmas present he'd gotten for her? She had never felt more pain, more disappointment. She'd been on cloud nine for two days feeling like her life as an artist had finally begun and there was proof it had all been fake. An art collector hadn't seen her talent and bought her stuff. Ian had bought it so she could move in with him. The sense of betrayal tasted like copper in her mouth. There was nothing for it—she would do what she'd told Ian she would do if he dared buy one of her sculptures.

She would never see him again.

IAN LOVED HIS FATHER. He really did. And one thing he loved about his father was his speeches. They were equal parts entertaining and long-winded. And tonight

Ian knew the speech would be especially long as his father had decided—without telling him—to run for the US House of Representatives instead of for reelection as a state senator.

Well.

Good for Dad. Meanwhile, Ian needed Flash's body and he needed it five minutes ago.

While everyone else in the room was laughing at a particularly funny but good-natured jab at the governor, Ian slipped quietly out of the room and up the stairs. He'd been on edge all night as Flash met his extended family. The last time Flash had come to an Asher party it had ended in disaster. He'd told his entire family before she arrived that he was dead serious about this woman, and if anyone even stepped one toe out of line around her, this would be the last Asher party they'd be getting an invitation to. And every last one of them had behaved perfectly, treating Flash like she was already one of the family. He hoped by this time next year she would be.

Thoughts of their future together put a smile on his face as he snuck up to the second floor, looked around for any party stragglers and then strode to the door of his childhood bedroom.

When he opened the door he didn't find Flash in his bed like he'd hoped. Although there was a woman in his room.

"Oh, my God..." he breathed as he walked around the metal sculpture that stood over five feet tall.

This was Flash's sculpture of his mother. It had to be. The piece was ivy vines that had been sculpted into the shape of a woman's body, one arm extended as if reaching for something or someone. Vines as veins. One long

vine ran from the bottom of the woman's left heel all
the way up to the neck. And it was that central core of
steel, the spine, that anchored the entire sculpture. He
could see through the various leaves at the hollow core
of the sculpture. But it wasn't entirely hollow. Where
the woman's heart should be was a single ivy leaf hanging from a metal chain suspended in the chest cavity.
Engraved on the leaf was one word—*Ian.*

"It's your mother, isn't it?"

Ian spun around and found his father standing in
the doorway.

"Yeah," Ian said. "It is. This is Flash's sculpture?"

His father nodded. "You told me to go to the gallery
to see your girlfriend's art. I did. I wasn't expecting…"
He stood in front of the sculpture as if to look the
woman in her ivy eyes. "I wasn't expecting this."

"It's… I knew she was good, but I didn't know she
was this good," Ian said. He felt like someone had
punched him in the throat. He could hardly speak.

"I saw your name written on the heart," his father
said softly, his voice choked with emotion, "and I had
to leave the room for a few minutes."

Ian blinked back tears.

"You bought this?" Ian asked.

"I did. For you. For us. For our family. I want this
in our family."

"Flash said an art collector from Seattle bought this.
She was so happy."

"I didn't want you knowing I'd bought it. It would
have ruined the surprise. I saw you two sneaking up
here. I wanted to catch you before you saw your Christmas present. I guess I was too late."

"A little. I…" Ian walked around the sculpture again.

"She called me her muse. She told me to give her an idea for a piece, and I said I wanted something of my mother since I never got to know her. I never imagined she'd do this."

"I never stopped loving her," his father said. "Even after all these years it still feels like an open wound. I shouldn't have cut you off from her family. When she died...when the accident happened, she was coming back to me. She'd taken you to her parents' house and I called and begged and begged for her to come back. And she wanted to come back but she wasn't sure yet. She left you with her parents and she was on her way to meet me, to talk it out with me. She died coming back to me."

"Dad..."

"And your grandparents, her parents, they did not want to give you back to me. I just lost my wife, and I was facing the possibility of losing my baby boy, too? We fought. It was an ugly fight."

"They filed for custody?"

"They did. I won, but you lost. I blamed them for a long time for her death. That was unfair of me. My parents were as unhappy with us eloping as her parents were. And then I punished you by keeping you away from your grandparents because I couldn't forgive them for trying to take you from me. I spent too many years seeing Ivy's parents as the enemy instead of what they really were—my son's family."

"Dad, don't you think you should be downstairs talking to the reporters?"

"You are more important. This is more important." He pointed at the sculpture. "I want you to contact your grandparents. They're still alive. I have their phone number, their address. They should see this sculpture. They should know their grandson and his girlfriend who made it. I have everything down in my office. Whenever you're ready, I'll give it all to you. And I hope you can forgive me for being so selfish with you the past thirty-five years. It was hard to forgive the people who tried to take my son from me. It was too easy to think about my own pain and my own grief instead of remembering they'd lost their daughter and were acting out of pain and grief just like I was. I don't know if they'll forgive me, but they'll love you and that's all that matters to me."

"I don't know what to say."

"Nothing to say. I was wrong. And you know how hard it is for a politician to say he's wrong."

"Christmas miracle."

"And all thanks to your lovely lady. Where is she, by the way? I want to thank her for this."

"I don't know." Ian stuck his head into the hallway. "I wanted to give her the Christmas gift I got her so I sent her up here..."

Flash would have done what he asked. She would have come to his bedroom. She would have seen the sculpture. And he'd told her he'd gotten her a big Christmas gift...

And she would have been fucking furious at him because the only thing she told him not to do was buy one of her sculptures. He hadn't, but his dad had.

"Oh, fuck," Ian said with a groan.

"Ian!"

"Dad, I have to go," he said.

"Go? Where?"

"I have to find Flash."

"She was just here."

"I know my girlfriend. She saw this and ran."

"Why?"

"Because she told me to never buy any of her art."

"You didn't buy it. I did."

"Yes, but she doesn't know that. I need to find her."

"Well, find her. I have a Christmas gift for her."

"Dad, I don't think she'll—"

"She'll want it. I promise. Go get your lady. Do whatever you have to do to get her back. Trust me on that."

Ian didn't walk out of the room. He ran. He ran out of the bedroom, down the hall, down the stairs, and hopped in his dad's Prius since it was easier to get to than his own car. And his father said he should do whatever it takes to get Flash back. Surely that included grand theft auto.

He drove as fast as he safely could to Flash's apartment complex. He ran up to her door and knocked.

And knocked.

And knocked.

Nothing.

He ran back down the stairs and knocked on Mrs. Scheinberg's door.

He hated doing it. It was after ten and he assumed she was already asleep, but if Flash had come home, Mrs. Scheinberg would probably have heard her truck.

The door opened two inches only and Ian saw Mrs. Scheinberg peeking through the gap over the door chain.

"Ian? What on earth?"

She closed the door and opened it all the way.

"Flash isn't here, is she?" he asked without further preamble.

"No, why would she be? She went to the party."

"She did come and then she left. She won't answer my phone calls or return my messages. Long story."

"You weren't mean to her, were you? Or your family?"

"No, I swear. It's just a misunderstanding. A bad one, but still, it'll be fine as soon as she talks to me."

"You know she has her pride."

"Yeah, I know, I know. Too much pride. I better go. I have to find her. Any idea where she'd be? Any idea at all?"

"Try 7212 Northeast Prescott."

"That is a really specific answer," Ian said.

"It's her workshop," she said. "If she's not there, then I have no idea where she is. But she's there."

"You're sure?"

"It's where she went after she was kicked out of your last party."

"We're going to get this party thing right eventually."

"You better. I don't have a lot of years left and I better see a wedding before I go."

"I promise," Ian said. "You can be my best man. Best woman."

"I'll hold you to that."

He kissed her cheek and headed back into Portland. On the way to Prescott, Ian called upon his mother's faith and his father's and prayed Flash was there. If she wasn't at the workshop, he had no idea where she could be. She had other friends she could have run to and stayed with and it could be days or weeks before he saw her again. He tried to tamp down the apocalyptic thinking. It was just a misunderstanding. It was just a mistake. He wasn't going to be like his father in twenty years still kicking himself for losing the woman he loved.

He pulled into the driveway of a weedy little green house with a hand-painted sign in the front window that read Studios for Rent. When he stepped out of the car he heard the unmistakable sparking sound of a MIG welding torch.

Ian knew he had to be careful if he didn't want to take a torch burn to his face. He didn't knock on the side door but simply slipped quietly inside and moved a safe distance from Flash's worktable. She'd changed out of her dress and into canvas work pants and a white tank top. The dress hung on a hook behind the door. She'd wrapped it in plastic to keep it safe.

While he waited for her to acknowledge his presence, he glanced around the shop. He saw the mold she'd used to create the ivy leaves for the sculpture of his mother. She amazed him with what she could do with her mind and her muscle and her imagination.

Flash finally killed her arc and sat her welding gun down on the table. She raised the visor of her helmet and turned around to face him.

"What?" she asked. That was all. One word. What?

"What are you working on?"

"Nothing," she said.

"Sounded like something."

"Practicing a new technique I saw online. I'm playing with scraps. It's fun when you don't have to worry about screwing up."

"You're the only woman I know who would call practicing MIG welding techniques on scrap metal 'fun.' No, let me correct that. You're the only person I know of any gender who would say that."

"Not my fault you don't know as many cool people as I do."

Ian took a step toward her. She didn't say anything to stop him so he took another.

"Are you going to ask why I'm here?"

"No," she said. "But I'm guessing you're going to tell me."

"I am. But first, did you like your Christmas present I gave you?"

"No, I didn't."

"Why not?"

"Because I told you if you bought one of my sculptures, I would never talk to you again, and you did it, anyway, because that's what people like you do—whatever you want because you can and everyone else's feelings be damned."

Ian pointed at the dress hanging on the hook behind the door. "That's your Christmas gift. I bought the dress from Mrs. Scheinberg for you."

"You what?"

"I bought you that dress. She even gave me a discount as long as I promised to go to shul with her. That's your Christmas gift from me. Not the sculpture. My father bought your sculpture. I had no idea he'd bought it and no idea he'd stored it in my old room when I sent you up there. I was as shocked to see it as you were."

"Your dad bought it?"

"You were right. He wasn't thrilled we were dating. He's a politician. Image is everything to them, and you made him a little nervous. I admit all of that. But my father is a good guy ninety-nine percent of the time, and when I told him he should go check out your work at the gallery, he did. He saw the sculpture and fell in love with it. He bought it to keep in the family."

Flash crossed her arms over her chest and leaned back against the worktable.

"You told him to go look at my art."

"I was showing you off," Ian said. "I wanted him to see how talented you are. And he saw. He said he had to leave the room for a few minutes when he noticed you'd engraved my name on the heart."

"I did that because I know your name was engraved on your mother's heart."

"I'm sure it was," Ian said.

"And I know that because it's engraved on mine."

"Flash..." Ian couldn't speak anymore.

"It hurt more than anything ever hurt when I thought you'd betrayed my trust," she said. "I felt that hurt all the way to my heart. It's terrifying to love someone as much as I love you. I was looking for any excuse to get away from how much I love you. You gave me one."

"Cutting your losses again?" he asked.

She nodded. "Yeah. I guess I need to stop doing that."

"I'd appreciate it."

She dug her hands in her pockets. She looked small and young, hurt.

"My mom was a hotel housekeeper when she met my father," Flash said. "She'd started cleaning motels and worked her way up to a five-star hotel in Seattle. He was the sort of guy who stayed in five-star hotels."

"Rich?"

She nodded. "And he was the sort of man who used women because he thought the whole world was a banquet, and he was the guest of honor. I'm sure you know the type."

"Very well, unfortunately."

"Mom got in touch with him when she found out she was pregnant. He refused to have anything to do with her or me. He sent her a check for ten thousand dollars and wrote 'Final Payment' on the memo line."

"Asshole."

"Seriously. When I was nine I asked Mom about who my father was and why he never visited or called or anything. Mom doesn't like to lie or sugarcoat stuff. She said, 'Your father doesn't think we're good enough for him.' I feel like it's coded in my DNA now, this distrust of men with money or power and especially both. And that's shitty, right? Taking all that old pain that has nothing to do with you out on you?"

"You and my dad have a lot in common. You're both punishing yourselves over things you didn't have any control over. He didn't cause the car accident that killed my mother. You didn't cause your father to reject you before you were even born. And yet, decades later, you're both still beating yourselves up over it. Dad won't get remarried and you keep running from me."

She rubbed her bare arms and shrugged. "I don't want to be like this," she said.

"I know. But I love you, anyway. And I'm not going to stop loving you. I'm going to love you long enough and hard enough that you eventually figure out that I'm not one of the bad guys. I understand it might take a while but you're worth waiting for."

"Are you mad at me?" she asked.

"For what? Doing exactly what you told me you'd do?"

"I jumped to conclusions. I should have talked to you instead of running."

"I should have talked to you before I broke up with

you. So I can't really blame you for doing the same damn thing I did. I'm just glad you didn't weld truck nuts to my bumper again."

"How do you know I didn't?" she asked.

"Oh, my God, did you?" He winced. Flash laughed and it was the sweetest sound he'd heard all night.

"No," she said. "Only because I don't have any on me. But the thought did occur to me."

"If you ever weld truck nuts to my car again…"

"What?" she asked, lifting her chin defiantly.

Ian walked over to her table and took her into his arms.

"I'll fuck you," he said. "And you'll like it."

"That's not much of a threat."

"I'll take any excuse to fuck you," he said.

"I'm here. You're here. Is that enough of an excuse for you?"

"More than enough." He reached for her but she held up her hand to stop him.

"What?"

"Do the thing," she said.

"The thing? Oh, yeah, the thing."

Ian ripped his bow tie off and threw it on the floor.

"Okay," she said breathlessly. "Now you can fuck me."

12

THE TABLES WERE covered with equipment and the floor was littered with metal shards and grease. They had no other choice but to fuck against the one clean patch of wall. Ian pushed her back to the wall and pulled her pants and underwear down to her ankles. He groaned when he entered her, and so did she. She groaned in ecstasy but also in relief that even though she'd left him, he'd come for her. And she knew as he lifted her leg and wrapped it around his back he would always come for her. Ian took her mouth with a hard deep kiss and Flash wound her arms around his neck. He fucked her with quick rough thrusts to drive the point home that she was his, all his, and always would be his as long as she wanted.

"More, Ian," she said, and he lifted her off her feet and buried his cock deep inside her. She arched her back to take it all and he pumped his hips to give it all. They were a writhing mass of mouths and tongues and arms and legs and sweaty hair and grasping hands. Ian bruised her back with his thrusts and she didn't care. She loved it. She wanted it. The harder he gave it to her, the harder she wanted it. They could be tender with each other later tonight, in Ian's bed, which would soon be their bed. Right now she just wanted him so deep inside her she would feel him all the way into her blood, her bones, her DNA.

"I love you," she said against his lips, into his kisses. "I love you…" She said it until she came with a sudden sharp spike of pleasure all the way from her stomach to her toes. She said it again when Ian came inside her, filling her and filling her as she clung to his shoulders and wished she never had to let him go.

Ian took a breath, pressed his forehead to hers.

"You feel better now?" he asked.

"Yes. You?"

"Much better."

"I should have been wearing my dress," she said. "It's much sexier than my work clothes. And knowing Mrs. Scheinberg, she fully expects me to seduce you while I'm wearing it."

"I love the dress," Ian said. "And I love you in it. But truth is, you're sexier to me in your work clothes than anything else. Except naked."

"You really do love me, don't you?" she asked.

"You just figuring that out?"

"Yes," she said.

"You'll get used to it. Now get dressed. We have to go back to the party. Dad has a present for you."

"Any other orders?" she asked as he let her down to the floor.

"Yes," he said. "One more order."

"And that is?"

He took her face in his hands and looked her deep in the eyes.

"Never, ever weld truck nuts to my car again."

Flash sighed in defeat.

"Yes, boss."

"One more order."

"What?"

"Never, ever run away from me again," he whispered. "Please?"

"Well," she said, putting her hands over his. "Since you said 'please.'"

Flash pulled herself together as best she could and Ian zipped her back into her dress. They returned to the party and found it still in full swing.

"Where have you two been?" Angie asked when she and Ian walked back in the front door.

"Went for a walk," Flash said. "Got a little overheated in the house."

"A walk? For over an hour?" Angie asked.

"Nice night," Ian said. "Where's my father?"

"Upstairs," Angie said as she casually wiped red lipstick off Ian's ear with her cocktail napkin.

"Um, thank you," Flash said, blushing.

"Glad you had a nice 'walk,'" Angie said with a wink before strolling away to the bar.

"I really do like your family," Flash said. "They're not at all what I expected."

"They're pretty cool," Ian said as they walked up the stairs in pursuit of his father. "I'll keep them. I might be getting more family soon."

"Somebody pregnant?"

"No. But thanks to your sculpture of my mother, Dad finally talked to me about my other family, my mom's family. And he told me he wants me to contact them."

"That's amazing, Ian."

"I can't wrap my mind around it. For years I was afraid to ask him about my mother's family. I didn't want to hurt him by bringing all that old pain up again. And then tonight we were looking at your sculpture and he just started talking about her. All thanks to you."

"That's the power of art. It can get through any chinks, any seams, and if there aren't any, it'll make them," she said, smiling up at him. He stopped them on the landing to kiss her but the kiss didn't get very far.

"Finally. About damn time you two turned up." Ian's father stood at the top of the stairs. A woman with dark brown skin and dark eyes wearing a burgundy-and-gold sari stood next to him.

"Is this her?" the woman asked, her words tinged with a subtle Indian accent.

"Ms. Veronica Redding, please meet Ms. Hema Lalwani. She owns a gallery in Seattle."

Flash was too nervous to speak. Everyone even remotely familiar with the art scene in the Pacific Northwest knew of Hema Gallery in Seattle. Flash had gone to every exhibit there in the past four years.

"You're very gifted, Ms. Redding," Ms. Lalwani said. "I've never seen metal sculpting as intricate as yours on such a large scale. I'd like to feature your work in my gallery next winter."

"That's very nice of you," Flash said. "But I'm afraid I can't accept your offer. You're obviously friends with my boyfriend's father and I can't—"

"You misunderstand," Ms. Lalwani said. "I have never met Mr. Asher before in my life. I came here because after your piece sold, the owner of the Morrison sent me photographs of your work. I contacted Mr. Asher about the piece as I wished to see it in per-

son. He invited me here to this party. I am not offering
you a gallery showing as a favor to anyone other than
me and my gallery. You should say yes."

"I don't know," Flash said. "The only reason you
heard about my piece was because my boyfriend's father bought it."

"Young lady," Ms. Lalwani said with a tight smile
that didn't look like a smile. "My job is to discover
new artists. Usually the artists are the ones sending me
photographs of their work or begging me to see it or
even meet with them for five minutes. I don't care who
bought the piece. I don't care who sent me the photographs of your work. I saw them, I was intrigued. That
is why I am here. I had never heard of Dean Asher before Friday. I don't care who he is. I certainly don't care
who your boyfriend is. I don't even care who you are,
Ms. Redding. I only care about art, your art, and I want
it in my gallery."

"Damn," Ian said under his breath.

"I think I'm in love with you," Flash said.

Ms. Lalwani looked upward and gave a little elegant shrug.

"You aren't the first to tell me that."

"She accepts," Ian said. "Right, Flash?"

"Right," Flash said. "I accept."

"Flash?" Ms. Lalwani said. "Is that your name?"

"Nickname. There was this movie—"

"Yes, *Flashdance*," Ms. Lalwani said. "I know it.
Who doesn't?"

"He's never seen it," Flash said, pointing her thumb
over her shoulder at Ian.

"Never?" Ms. Lalwani said. "You'll have to correct
that oversight. Now come with me. We need to talk

about the show. I'll need new pieces. At least three. Your technical proficiency is on display in your floral pieces but those are representational. Only your sculpture of the woman in ivy is true art. That is what you should be doing."

Flash's heart leaped and her brain danced and she felt like she'd been struck by lightning. Everything Ms. Lalwani said made sense. She could see it, what she'd been doing wrong, what she'd finally gotten right. It was electric, speaking to someone who understood her art and could help her.

"You're right," Flash said. "You're absolutely right. I knew it while I was making it. I knew I'd finally figured out my motif."

"You two can use my private office," Dean Asher said. "Across the hall on the right."

"Thank you, Mr. Asher," Ms. Lalwani said.

"It's Senator Asher actually."

"I don't care."

"Will you have dinner with me tomorrow?" he asked.

Ms. Lalwani raised her eyebrow at him.

"A *state* senator?"

"Running for US Congress," he said.

"Hmm. Win your seat, then I'll consider it. Come with me, Flash." Ms. Lalwani waved her hand and walked away.

"Well," Dean Asher said. "That went better than I expected. Good luck with her." He paused to kiss Flash's cheek on his way down the stairs. "Put in a good word for me."

"Better go talk to the lady," Ian said. "I don't think she's the sort who likes to be kept waiting."

"She's so famous."

"I've never heard of her."

"You've also never seen *Flashdance*. She married an American billionaire, and he died and now she's, like, the most famous art collector in the world. And her gallery is known for launching important young artists. I am..." She started to spike up her hair but Ian stopped her.

"Stay calm. You got this," he said.

"Tell your dad I said thank you," Flash said,

"I absolutely will. I told you that you were good."

"You did. But there's a big difference between knowing you're good and knowing you're good enough," she said.

"You're good enough," he said. "You're incredible."

She kissed him again for love and for luck, and she knew she'd have plenty of both as long as they were together.

"Okay, go knock 'em dead," he said.

"I can do that." She let go of his hand and started up the stairs. "It's just so embarrassing, you know."

"What is?"

"I met the most important gallery owner in the region, and the entire time we were talking about art, my boyfriend's fly was down."

"It was? Shit." Ian looked down at his pants and up at her with a scowl. A very sexy scowl.

Flash laughed and laughed all the way up the stairs. "Made you look!"

* * * * *

HARLEQUIN®

A *Romance* FOR EVERY MOOD™

Stay up-to-date on all your
romance-reading news with the
Harlequin Shopping Guide,
featuring bestselling authors, exciting new
miniseries, books to watch and more!

The newest issue will be delivered right to you
with our compliments! There are 4 each year.

Signing up is easy.

EMAIL

ShoppingGuide@Harlequin.ca

WRITE TO US

HARLEQUIN BOOKS
Attention: Customer Service Department
P.O. Box 9057, Buffalo, NY 14269-9057

OR PHONE

1-800-873-8635 in the United States
1-888-343-9777 in Canada

Please allow 4-6 weeks for delivery of the first issue by mail.

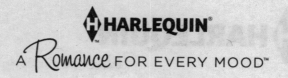

HARLEQUIN®

A *Romance* FOR EVERY MOOD™

JUST CAN'T GET ENOUGH?

Join our social communities
and talk to us online.

You will have access to the latest
news on upcoming titles and special
promotions, but most importantly,
you can talk to other fans about your
favorite Harlequin reads.

Harlequin.com/Community

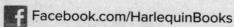 Facebook.com/HarlequinBooks

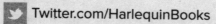 Twitter.com/HarlequinBooks

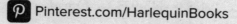 Pinterest.com/HarlequinBooks

HSOCIAL

HARLEQUIN®

A *Romance* FOR EVERY MOOD™

Love the Harlequin book you just read?

Your opinion matters.

Review this book on your favorite book site, review site, blog or your own social media properties and share your opinion with other readers!

Be sure to connect with us at:
Harlequin.com/Newsletters
Facebook.com/HarlequinBooks
Twitter.com/HarlequinBooks

Turn your love of reading into rewards you'll love with

Harlequin My Rewards

**Join for FREE today at
www.HarlequinMyRewards.com**

Earn **FREE BOOKS** of your choice.

Experience **EXCLUSIVE OFFERS** and contests.

Enjoy **BOOK RECOMMENDATIONS**
selected just for you.

PLUS! Sign up now
and get **500** points
right away!

Earn
FREE
REWARDS
HarlequinMyRewards.com
Join
Today!

MYR16R

Her bikini panties were pale blue, resting high on each cheek, just far enough to make him catch his breath. On top, he spotted the straps of her matching bra poking out from underneath a cascade of thick auburn hair.

He wondered what she looked like from the front…

She turned quickly, probably hearing his irregular breathing.

Now her scream was definitely of the "help, I'm being assaulted" variety.

He lowered the crowbar, noticing the two large suitcases behind her. "Hey," he said softly. "I'm not going to hurt you."

She waved her cell phone at him as she grabbed the nearest thing at hand—a pillow—and held it up against her semi-naked body. "I've already hit my panic button. The police will be here any minute."

"Good," he said, leaning his weapon against the door frame, trying hard to ignore the fact that she was hot. Certainly way too hot for that douchebag, Wes. "I'm anxious to hear you explain what you're doing in my apartment."

"*Your* apartment? You mean you own the one below?"

He nodded. "It's all one unit."

"But I have a key. And five days left on the rental agreement."

"What agreement?"

"My…" Her pause was notable, mostly for the look of fury that passed across her face. "My jerkface former business partner rented this place from the— From you, I guess. But I didn't think you lived here."

"Huh. Well, I think you might have been misinformed by Jerkface. I'm assuming you mean Wes Holland?"

Her whole demeanor changed from fierce guardedness to utter defeat. "Wait a minute. How do I know you're the real owner?"

"I understand you must be angry," he said, "but that doesn't change the fact that you'll have to leave."

"What? *Now?*"

"Well, no." It was already late, and he couldn't see himself throwing her out. "First thing tomorrow."

*Pick up DARING IN THE CITY by Jo Leigh,
available in January 2017 wherever you buy
Harlequin® Blaze® books.*

www.Harlequin.com

Luca didn't get back to his new place until just after 8:00 p.m. It had turned blustery, and he rubbed his cold hands together as he entered the elevator.

Finally. He had his own apartment. Tomorrow his king bed and wide-screen TV would be delivered.

Ten minutes later he thought he heard the buzzer, but no way was the pizza he ordered here that fast. A moment later a scream rang out.

He grabbed the crowbar sitting on a pile of rags, his heart racing. It occurred to him that the scream didn't sound like a "help, I'm being assaulted" scream.

He moved closer to the door. Another scream, this time louder.

It was coming from inside his apartment.

Luca glanced up the stairs. Goddamn Wes Holland hadn't moved out. Or he had, but he'd left a woman behind.

Cursing, he started up the staircase. As he moved stealthily down the hallway he heard her shouting. "Bastard" came in the clearest, followed by a wail.

He waited at the edge of the door, finally able to hear her words.

"How the hell does promising to pay me back do me any good?"

The tears and desperation came through loud and clear.

"That was all my savings," she said. "I hate you. You're such a coward, you won't even pick up."

Luca assumed the woman was talking about Wes and leaving him a voice mail. Had he really run off with her money?

He risked peeking inside the room. Luckily, the woman had her back to him. Lucky for him because it was a very nice view: the woman was wearing nothing but underwear.

Very tiny underwear.

REQUEST YOUR FREE BOOKS!
2 FREE NOVELS PLUS 2 FREE GIFTS!

HARLEQUIN®

Blaze

red-hot reads!